RAVEN HEART

MAGIC AND MAGE SERIES EPISODE 4

ANGHARAD THOMPSON REES

PROLOGUE

One second. One breath. One spell.

Emrysa's ruby lips snarled in a half smile, watching as the two Cheval sisters raised their magic-filled palms.

Mocking laughter rose to her throat; *as if they could harm me now.* Now that she was returned. Now that she was... flesh. But the laugh did not erupt. Instead, it caught in Emrysa's throat, and in that split second, everything changed.

Camelot's vast hall lost its echoing acoustics. The army behind the dragon heart, the handsome men at Emrysa's side, Merlin and King Arthur, corrupted under her blackened spell, all of them—everything—blurred from her vision. She saw only the intent behind the sisters' spell, and it made her half-heart pound.

"Now!" yelled Amara and Fae in unison.

They braced their palms forward, surging white light exploding from fingertips. Like lightning rods, the white crackled, tendrils joining, growing. Reaching.

Emrysa had time only to stagger back two shuffling steps, bumping into King Arthur's throne in the process. Had she not been so concerned about the spell's intent, she would have prepared a counter spell. But she froze. Fear—a paralyzing poison, trickling through her veins.

The white light found its way to her, wrapping itself around Emrysa's body, pulling her into itself. A blinding whiteness. Surging. *Purging*.

Emrysa did not see the army of witches, the red-headed Hemeth, or the sisters shield their eyes from the exploding whiteness. But she felt it all. And with everything she had, she fought as the spell grappled at her mind, her thoughts, her *soul*.

A scream erupted, internal, a high-pitched howl serenading a million memories and emotions lived and hid beneath the surface of Emrysa's mind. Locked away. Moments too black to recall. Hopelessness too desperate to conceive. All of it came back, flooding through her veins. Emrysa writhed under the white hold —the truth spell—reliving the nightmares she had so painstakingly packed away into oblivion. And as if emotional pain alone could kill, the witch so feared for centuries, dropped to her knees and wept.

"Stop!" Emrysa sobbed; a howl wrenched from the deepest pit of despair. "Stop, *stop.*"

Her plea sounded like a prayer.

Fae and Amara stared open-mouthed as the witch they so despised, their aunt—Morganne's jailor—rocked upon her knees, gripping her head with strained fingers. Emrysa released a haunting wail as she swayed, sharp nails clawing into her own temples, drawing blood. She stopped, only to pound her fists at her forehead, fighting her thoughts away.

But they did not stop the spell.

The sisters stood, and they waited, while Emrysa screamed at the truth forced upon her. And from her mouth, it came. Like a mist at first, then taking shape and mass, painting the hall in a thick, glossy white. This whiteness spread to create walls around the witch and the two sisters until there was nothing and no-one— silence. Even the witch Emrysa's screams subsided to quiet sobs.

Weak, Emrysa struggled to her feet, gathering her breath and composure, though her eyes told the tale of her emotional disquiet.

"So, *nieces,* you have brought me to The Void." Emrysa's lips puckered as she nodded. "I'm impressed. I would not have thought you to know about such a time and space."

Fae and Amara dared a glance at one another. They wanted the truth; the open, honest truth, but the emptiness of The Void was indeed a surprise, even to them. And somehow, with the cruel smirk spreading across Emrysa's ruby lips like a bloody slash, she seemed to pick up on this. She turned, and walked away, though no matter how many paces she took from them, the distance never changed. It was as if the white walls were as far away as an impossible horizon and yet held them together in the tight space.

Emrysa raised her arms overhead and Fae followed the line of her fingers as they reached for the sky. A sky that was white and empty, faraway and close. Fae stepped forward and the ground beneath her feet, though solid, rippled like water—each ripple reaching out as far as the eye could see into nothing.

This was a desolate space.

But Fae was not afraid, though she breathed into her dragon heart for extra courage. "We have brought you here for the truth, Emrysa."

"You don't say?!" Emrysa replied to her willowy blond niece, wearing torn rags fit only for a scullery maid.

Amara scowled, hating the way Emrysa moved,

knowing Morganne was inside her somewhere, some-how, and, feeling responsible for the sister she had lost, the thought of war and darkness dissipated in the cold, white nothing. "Tell me, *tell us,* how do we get Morganne back? I demand you tell me the truth. Now."

Emrysa barked a mirthless sound before returning to her mockingly sweet mask of concern. Yet, the slight tremble to her fingers, the slight watering of her midnight black eyes, exposed a gentle vulnerability. She lifted her right hand and wagged her finger.

"No, no, no, my dear, senseless little witches. The truth spell is not some childish game, you cannot demand I tell you one truth or another and I simply obey. That is not how The Void works—"

"Then tell us," Amara barked.

"This is *my* truth, you stupid girl," Emrysa roared, glaring at Amara, hating the way the young witch resembled her own appearance. "*I* have to relive *my* story, *my* truth. *Everything.*" She turned away as if making her way to leave, yet again, no matter how far she paced, no further could she go in The Void's expanse. "To know the truth, you must see everything that lead us to this place. Truth has edges, sides, hidden layers and secret pathways. Truths have riddles and lies and deceits—a multitude of sins have been created in the name of truth, though very few discover the reality of it.

"So you see, I cannot *tell* you the truth. You have to live it, live in my memories, my *life.* Hence The Void. No time. No space. Just you, here, to relive my story. To understand *my* truth."

A fox's grin spread across Emrysa's face, and she bowed with the practiced grace of a theatrical performer. "Welcome," she said, "to my life."

And The Void dissolved into nothing but thoughts and memories and a story that started a long, long time ago...

PART I

"Stories never really begin. They are an endless continuation of love and lies and choices. They extend—reaching both forward and back immeasurably. This is their charm. One can begin a story, yes, but you begin only at a start of a *part*. The rest, as they say, is history."

—Emrysa Cheval

1

THREE MOONS

*E*mrysa Cheval galloped along the corridor, raven hair streaming, her skirts bustling about her bare ankles. She giggled, the sound of summer cheer bouncing from the walls, and cast a backward glance over her shoulder.

Dermot gave chase, making ground with his long legs, his face wearing a strange hue of blue.

"I'll get you, sister! You'll pay for this, you iconic muttonhead!" he called, though the edges of his threat frayed with humor and, perhaps, a little admiration.

Emrysa kept running, grabbing fistfuls of her skirt's folds as she did. "You've never caught me yet!" She squealed and quickened her pace. Her younger brother —well, younger by about an hour—*was* getting faster, stronger too, but his magic was still no match for hers.

No match for anybody's. Everyone said so, and although Dermot sometimes believed his sister to be teasing and taunting him with her magical practical jokes, but they both knew what she was doing. Emrysa was trying to help, trying to encourage him to play. To feel magic as something fun and light, and not the heaviness their parents had pressed upon his shoulders.

It was simple.

All witches and wizards had an amount of magical ability—to cast, to manipulate the world around them. But there were other forms of magic, Emrysa knew. It wasn't that her brother was *bad* at magic, he was just yet to discover what magic would be his forte. He was yet to discover his True Ability. He preferred science. And perhaps, in and of itself, that *was* a form of magic.

Emrysa rounded the corner, gripping the wall as she did to keep her balance. She wouldn't run far. She never did. And her brother's pursuit would always end with the pair of them in breathless fits of laughter.

Emrysa *always* reversed her spells.

The blue hue to his face would dispel but, she hoped, the lesson would remain.

She burst through the double doors at the end of the corridor, where the low winter sun shimmered on frost-touched grass, sparkling at its touch. Barefooted, she picked up her pace in the open freedom, squealing at the coldness of her toes and checking over her shoulder to see Dermot close. Too close. Emrysa laughed with delight as he launched at her—the pair falling to the hard winter ground and tumbling down the hill toward the river, stopping only after a splash and an ice-cold watery embrace.

Dermot gasped as he burst to the surface, hair and goofy smile plastered to his face. "Emrysa!"

She laughed, wiping the cold water from her eyes and scrambling up the riverbank.

"Why didn't you use your magic to stop us from falling in?" Dermot almost shrieked whilst laughing through his chattering teeth. Even in the midst of summer, the Welsh water was barely a few degrees higher than freezing one's nether regions off, so with winter well and truly underway, the chill was almost unbearable.

Emrysa proffered a hand, helping her brother from the beautifully clear but frigid water. "Where is the fun in that? I like magic..." a wicked smile crept upon her face, "...but I *love* mischief!" And with that, she pushed Dermot back into the water, where he commenced his best water statue impression, complete with a rather impressive fountain streaming from his puckered lips. And without fail, his relentless good humor warmed Emrysa's bones under her sodden clothes.

For a moment, the pair almost forgot the truth of things.

This time, when Dermot scrambled up the riverbank to join Emrysa sitting against the old oak, she whispered a few words under her breath and dried their clothes in an instant. They stared out over the expansive view of wild countryside and ragged cliffs shaped by the turbulent coastline.

A mass of cloud hid the sun and the tips of the craggy mountains in the distance, just as a forced smile hid Emrysa's concerns.

"Out with it," Dermot said, looking not at the view now, but at his sister.

"Out with what?"

Dermot raised a brow, dragging his hand through his reddish hair the spell had dried but not tamed. "That pensive little look on those haughty features of yours." He wrapped an arm around her shoulder. He said these things, these mean things, but they both knew he never meant them. He loved playing the part of jester but Emrysa feared with their parents' hands weighing heavier on them more than ever, their days of fun and frivolity would soon be over.

It did not bode well in Emrysa's bones.

"It's all going to change, brother. I can *feel* it. Something. Something... I don't know. Just..." She trailed off, then turned away.

"You're worried because we're to come of age soon?"

"Only three moons," Emrysa said, resting her head on her brother's shoulders.

"And I suppose you're worried about getting that pretty face of yours all wrinkled and old and—*ow*!"

Dermot rubbed his smarting ribs and Emrysa gave him another dig for extra measure. "You're such an idiot at times, brother. No, I take it back. You're *always* an idiot."

"Just because you don't understand my alchemical equations, doesn't make them gibberish. Besides, it's better for others to think me a fool. At least that way, they don't expect much from me."

"Like they do me, you mean?"

Dermot shrugged. "Our parents expect so much from you because you keep showing them how capable you are."

"I'm not *that* capable," Emrysa said. "You know Mother has a blocking spell on her mind. Father has a... I don't know, like a prickly something around his thoughts and aura, I can't get close, I can't tell what's going on anymore. They're hiding something. Something big. And I feel like it all has to do with our eighteenth birthday."

"Oh! Come on, Miss Worrisome. They're probably just sick and tired of you probing their minds for secrets. You might be a powerful young witch, but you are also an incessantly nosy, mind-trespassing little wench."

Emrysa laughed. *Perhaps.* Perhaps he was right, but her bones were not often wrong, and they rang out now like a chorus of worried birds warning of a brewing storm to come.

"Come," Dermot said, pulling his sister to her feet. "Let's get back to the laboratory, and I can show you that wormhole I've been trying to create. It really is something. And perhaps, on the way, you could undo this spell from my blue face?"

Emrysa smiled, somehow forgetting about the blue hue on his features under the heavy cloud of concern for their unknown future. With a click of her fingers, she reversed her spell, and everything went back to normal.

But for how long? she wondered, looking up at the pale winter sky. Three moons. Three moons until *everything* would change.

Beside her, Dermot gasped. "The Council?"

Emrysa frowned, straining her eyes to better see in the distance.

For a while she remained silent, waiting, watching, as the caravan of midnight black horses meandered along the rolling hillside. And even though they were hours away by the dots they made on the far horizon, Emrysa could still make out the purple and gold tapestries—the Council's standard—fluttering from poles carried by leading riders. Casting a seeing spell, Emrysa caught sight of the somber stares and bleak auras around the Council members. A darkened cloud blotted the sun, concealing the land in shadows, and every bone in Emrysa's body screamed one word.

Run.

2

ICE AND SPITE

*E*mrysa raced along the corridors to the main hall.

"Mistress Cheval, is something afoot?" a guard called after her, but she ignored him, ignored *all* her father's men of arms as she galloped to the double doors and burst through, heart heaving.

Both Lord and Lady Cheval jumped at her entrance, her father rising to his feet in an instant.

"Dear child, whatever has happened?" he demanded, no concern in his voice, only fury, as always.

She tried to gather her thoughts, tried to calm her breath as she paced the large hall embellished with tapestries and winter decorations; ivy, holly, mistletoe. Father's impatience rose as Emrysa spluttered words unformed. He charged toward her, seizing her arms and shook her for answers.

"Whatever is it, child?" he roared.

"The Council," she said, breathless. "The Alchive Council are on their way."

Mother's chair clattered behind her as she as she shot to her feet. She cursed, muffling the words behind a quivering hand clasped to her mouth.

Father's jaw hung, his grip loosened, and though he continued to hold Emrysa, the pallor in his cheeks faded.

"The Council?" he repeated in a faraway whisper. His ice blue eyes stared through hers, into thoughts, into memories, and whatever surfaced suddenly brought him back to life. He dropped her arms, face stern once more. "Where? Where are they?"

"A few hours away, no more," Emrysa said, pointing to the window. Father stormed toward it, looking out across the rugged land shaped by coastal winds and storms. And there they were, dots on the horizon. They looked so small, so insignificant, but they were anything but.

"Where's Dermot?" Mother pressed, her voice hesitant, like the small unsure steps she took toward her daughter. Any concerns Emrysa had, multiplied. *What are they hiding? Why are they so afraid?*

Dermot finally caught up, standing beside his sister.

Father pointed a finger at each of them in turn. "You must not be seen by the Council, do you hear me?" There was so much venom in his voice, so much anger. Emrysa found her own anger prickling. After all, it's not like they had done anything wrong. No illegal spells or dangerous curses. The Alchive were known to judge by a heavy hand, but only when deserved, surely?

"Why are they coming?" Emrysa asked.

Father shot her a furious look but instead of flinching, Emrysa set her shoulders square. Raised her chin, defiant.

"It's got nothing to do with you," he growled.

Emrysa's dark eyes flicked to her mother, who had begun pacing.

"It has everything to do with them," Mother argued. Lord Cheval turned from his children to face his wife, and Mother's expression crumbled. Tears laced her eyes. "They come of age in three moons. Is there any wonder they would turn up so close to the time? Did you think they would forget? Miss them out? Ignore what is to come?"

"No, I did not believe that," Father raged. "I just... I hoped..." his voice softened. He sighed. "I thought we would have more time."

"More time for what?" Emrysa blurted.

Father strode to the long dining table, raising a goblet to his lips that stained them red. "It doesn't matter," he finally said, his voice void of emotion. "It doesn't matter now, what matters is what we do next. You let *me* deal with the Council. I don't want them to see you, hear you, or feel your presence. You hide, upstairs in that alchemy chamber of Dermot's and that's where you both stay until I call for you. Is that clear?"

"Yes, Father," Dermot muttered.

Emrysa raised an eyebrow.

"I'm warning you," Father threatened, glaring at her.

She rolled her eyes.

"Go on, go! Off with you. I'll see that the maids bring you dinner from the kitchens, but you will not dine here with us tonight. You will not dine with the Council members. Do you understand?"

"We understand," Dermot said through tight lips. Emrysa glared back at Father who was yet to blink. But this was a game Emrysa could play all day. He broke his stare first, shaking his head at her insolence.

"Promise to do as you're told," Mother began. "This is no time for your foolery, Emrysa. This is not a game. Promise."

Emrysa clenched her jaw with her silent reply, raising the color in her mother's cheeks and her temper, too. *What are they hiding?*

"Promise! Damn you, child!*"*

"I promise!" Emrysa finally spat, fingers crossed behind her back.

Father nodded, sending them on their way, and like scolded cats, they scampered from his presence.

Without a word, without a backward glance, the siblings rounded the corner until they were out of ear and eye shot from the guards and their parents.

"I don't suppose you intend to hide away in my chamber." Dermot didn't need a reply, which was good, because he didn't get one.

Instead, Emrysa came to a stop at a full-length window.

"What is it? What do you feel?" Dermot asked as she stared from the window, both hands pressed against the glass edged with ice and spite.

Emrysa braced herself, pushing her sight toward the black dots on the landscape, piercing space and time to get a better look. And something grappled at her, something pulled at her innards. She gasped.

Nature, Emrysa knew, holds its own power, its own magic, some of which cannot be altered or melded or wished into shape. Such as the magic of magnetism. A pulling and a repelling force. Emrysa felt an intoxicating degree of both as she focused on the Alchive Council riding toward their home under a cloud of subterfuge.

In equal parts she was repulsed by the very nature of the magical council—their cruel rules and disciplinarian demands; demands they would soon place upon her family for whatever reason. And whatever the reason, it wouldn't be good. The Council did not make social calls —everybody feared them or rather, feared their power. She felt—again—an instinctive urge to run, yet another part of her, a deep, deep down in her marrow part, felt only interest and curiosity and *something else* pulling her forward. Emrysa tried to ward off the effects but laws of nature are strong and unyielding, and her inner battle persisted.

"Six of them," Dermot counted, now that they were moving closer. "It's hardly an army."

"But it is enough," Emrysa said, tipping her head back toward the hall. "Come, the very least we can do is find a place to eavesdrop on our intrusive visitors."

Dermot smiled his roguish smile. "From you, my dear conniving sister, I would expect no less."

3

CRIMSON RED

*T*hey hid in the eaves. *A perfect place for eavesdropping;* Dermot had laughed at his own joke, which wasn't really a joke at all, not considering the circumstances. It appeared only two of the riders were Council members, the rest were guards—as if such powerful witches needed guards—and these guards waited in their cups in the ale room with the Cheval men of arms. The two Council members sat at the long wooden table with Lord and Lady Cheval, admiring with greedy eyes the Golden Oak at the center of the great room—the much talked about showpiece of the Cheval residence. The giant tree grew upwards and outwards, the castle built around to accommodate its thick, laden branches that never lost their leaves, even during the darkest days of winter solstice.

Both envied and revered (some believing this to be the source of the Cheval's covetous magical powers), the Golden Oak glimmered and shimmered as if aware of its own importance. Its leaves lit the faces of the two Alchive members, while the open fire roaring in the winter hearth cast tall shadows of branches along the castle walls behind them.

"They are so *young*," Emrysa whispered, watching the play of shadows and light upon their faces.

"And pretty," said Dermot, eyeing the pale-haired witch sat next to Father.

Emrysa rolled her eyes. And yet, her eyes *had* strayed more than once to the dark-haired, dark-skinned man, boy, no... something in between, who sat next to the silent witch. Pretty would not be the word she would use to describe *him*, but pretty handsome would do, though she suspected her description was doing him an injustice. But handsome is as handsome does, she considered, so only time would tell. For now, whilst silent, the description would sit, but how many times had young earls appeared at the same table since Emrysa was soon to came of age? Each looked so appealing until they spoke, and they all voiced the same rehearsed lines, devoting themselves entirely to her hand and her future, tempting her father with good family alliances and wealth that they did not need.

Thankfully, Father did not believe in marriage to progress the family (not that he needed to), he, like Emrysa, believed in something more. And there was something more between the silent pale-haired witch and the silent man-boy with the serious hazel eyes. It glimmered, an aura, a magic of some sorts Emrysa could not place. It hovered over the two Council members like a second skin, binding them.

"Your last born will come of age within three moons." The pale haired witch spoke, her voice light and dainty, like a fox trotting through snow. Emrysa heard her brother groan in pleasure at the sound.

"Careful," she whispered, "it's not very manly to swoon from the eaves to her feet. And she won't appreciate all that drool upon your lips soaking her in a shower of your adoration, either. Besides, she's clearly taken."

"As are you, sister," jibbed Dermot, noticing the intensity in which Emrysa watched the dark-haired boy.

Emrysa flicked a hand at her brother. It was not *the boy* she was looking at, but his aura, she told herself, repeating this in her mind and convincing herself a little more each time. All the while, a pulling attraction and a pushing repulsion teased at her from the pair glowing beneath the hearth light.

"Precautions need to be taken," the pale witch

continued. "Do you intend to procreate further? Do you intend to continue your bloodline with a newborn?"

"Of course!" Mother butted in, her face several shades paler than usual, eyes wider than before. "We have been trying for years, we have a..." she looked at Father, "... a fertility spell in place. We shall conceive again. You need not worry about our last born. We will have another."

Emrysa and Dermot shot a surprised look at one another in the eaves.

"Very well." The pale witch continued, cold as ice. "We have been instructed to stay until the third full moon—when you either conceive another child or your last born comes of age. If within that time you do not conceive, your last born's fate will be sealed, as you well know."

Emrysa and Dermot shot another look, this time, brows knotted. Dermot mouthed, *what are they talking about?* Emrysa shrugged, looking back as Mother whimpered and Father shifted uneasily in his chair. He cleared his throat before speaking. "We do not believe he possesses a dragon heart." There was a slight tremble to his usual strong tenor.

Emrysa and Dermot mouthed *dragon heart?* to one another, their brows thickening knots of unanswered questions before Father continued.

"Dermot's magic is third rate at best, we believe this bloodline, this... *fate,* will pass him."

Emrysa sensed her brother wilting at the callous comment and instinctively reached out to squeeze his hand. For extra measure, she whispered a soothing spell to help eradicate his upset. The exact moment she cast, the man-boy's hazel eyes darted up toward to eaves. They locked eyes. His face contorted and he held Emrysa in his hardened gaze. She shrank back, but it was too late. She was discovered. Found.

He feels my magic.

She tensed, remembering her father's warnings, the promise she made to her mother.

The man-boy's curious eyes flickered left to the pale-haired witch next to him. His lips twitched. Emrysa heard Dermot suck in air between his teeth. But in a flash, the man-boy's eyes were back on her. His aura, Emrysa noticed, turned from purple to pink to the bright red crimson of blood pulsing from a bleeding heart.

The pale witch placed a discrete hand upon the boy's thigh under the table, and looked not at him, but around him, noticing his changing aura.

"Merlin?" the pale haired witch asked. "You have sensed something?"

His eyes darted once more, ahead this time, looking

into nothing and giving nothing away. Emrysa and Dermot slunk further into the shadows.

"I..." he trailed off, turning to face the door in which they had entered. "I have a need to..." he stumbled to find his words, his excuse... his *lie.* "The horses. I need to check the horses."

He stood, steadying himself against the table. With his back to the pale witch, he glanced up once more, and Emrysa caught his hardening gaze and gulped.

The pale witch watched him go and placed a delicate finger to his lingering crimson aura, then brought the tip to her lips and licked. Dermot groaned in pleasure again while the pale witch frowned at her findings. She did not like the taste. Her face deadened, her pastel pink lips formed a tight line. When she spoke, she did so with distant thunder, defying her waif like form.

"You have three moons," promised the pale witch and with a tip of her head, she rose, following Merlin, leaving plates of half-finished food behind at the table. She stole a steely glance toward the eaves but found nothing.

Deep within the shadows under a concealment spell, Emrysa and Dermot watched as the pale witch left, and their strong, disciplinarian father buried his face in his hands and wept.

LUST AND FURY

*T*he pale witch's words still lingered in Emrysa's mind as she crept from her hiding place. *You have three moons.* But three moons 'til *what?* She considered asking her parents but already knew they would give her little knowledge about the Alchive Council's strange meeting. Besides, they were clearly hiding something from both her *and* Dermot by the spells wrapped tightly around their minds, stopping her probing or rummaging around their thoughts.

"Dragon hearts, fertility spells? What are the old biddies hiding?" Dermot asked as they crept from their vantage point.

"I think the better question is *why. Why* are they hiding it?" It was a deeper question, a layered question, and one which would not get answered by asking. Some answers, Emrysa mused, demanded to be discovered not told.

"You do know we have to follow them to find out what they're talking about," Emrysa said under her breath as they tried to walk nonchalantly past the guards lining the corridors.

Dermot turned his head toward the dining hall then back at Emrysa with a nervous smile. They nodded, and began to run, treading as softly as possible. Like whispers, they made no sound as they ran the length of the long winding corridors, stopping only to don their thick winter cloaks lined with wolf fur. They stepped out into the darkened early evening.

The moon was full and low in the star-strewn sky, a misty halo surrounding the orb lit the frost-touched grass with its gentle blue hue. Emrysa could easily see the footsteps made by the Alchive members—the trampled blades of grass from their weight and the secrets they carried.

The barn was close to the castle, nestled within a large copse of trees blackened by night, their skeletal branches swaying to the spiteful coastal breeze. Unseen, the ocean crashed against the cliffs below. The waves always sounded louder in the dark—a hypnotic and mesmerizing sound that helped soothe Emrysa's pounding heart and pulsating nerves as she noticed a gentle glow emanating from gaps within the wooden barn.

She cocked her head to the barn's direction. Dermot nodded, and they crept forward. The crunch of their footsteps on frost-laden ground was disguised by the chomping of hay and rustling of straw beneath horses' hooves within. Emrysa crouched, finding a hole within a knot of the wood to peer through, her brother following suit.

Emrysa first spied the majestic black horses glowing golden from the flaming light the dark-skinned boy held aloft. She concentrated on his aura. Not a spell as such. She was too worried to cast again after last time—he'd definitely felt her magic, she had no doubt. Though why he didn't call her out was another matter. So instead, she used her second sight. His crimson aura had melded back into the purple pulse of the witch, it pulled at him, softening the hard edges of his eyes and lips as if her aura somehow calmed him.

"You felt something in there, Merlin, at the table?" the pale witch asked.

Merlin stroked his sleek black horse with his fire-free hand and uttered nothing.

The pale witch laughed, but it sounded all... wrong. "Your aura, it turned *red*."

This, Emrysa knew, was not a statement. It was a

loaded question. Red auras, after all, had only two meanings—both so entangled it was impossible to interpret.

Lust and fury.

But why would the pale witch waste her time reading his aura? What insight would she glean from him that he wouldn't share as a fellow Council member? Emrysa leant forward, waiting for his answer, and Dermot gave her a little nudge in the ribs, shooting his brow up several times in quick succession and giving her a knowing wink. He mimicked an air-kiss, slobbering like a hound dog. She scowled and vowed silently to pay him back for that when they weren't in earshot, and this time it wouldn't only be his face she'd turn blue.

"I think it's wrong," Merlin said suddenly, breaking any thoughts of childish pranks.

The pale witch tutted. "It doesn't matter what you think. What matters is the safety of those under our care."

"But it's barbaric."

"And so too are dragons. We must exterminate them *before* they turn. This Dermot, or whatever his name is, *will* turn no matter what his parents believe. He's a Cheval. He is the last born. He is death and destruction incubated. He is Dragon Heart."

Emrysa and Dermot shot each other disbelieving

stares. Dermot, death and destruction incubated? What did that even mean? Little brother Dermot, who rolled his eyes and shook his head in disgust whenever Emrysa killed a pesky fly or spider in his presence. And dragon hearted? All Dermot was, was kind-hearted. None of this made sense.

"All I'm saying is that this practice has gone on for centuries," Merlin began. "Do we even know if dragon hearts turn these days? We find innocents guilty before any evidence or trial. And what about dragons being—"

"Don't," the pale witch warned. "I know what you're going to say. Don't."

She stepped closer to Merlin and placed her pale hand on his cheek. "The parents have concealment spells locking their thoughts. If they are hiding things from us, they are hiding them from their kin also. It will be easy to gain this Dermot's trust. And it's not like *we* have to kill him. We just give the orders."

Dermot stood and gasped, stepping away from the wooden barn as if her words pierced his skin—they certainly pierced Emrysa's heart—but the crunch of a dead branch snapping under his foot echoed in the silent pastures. Both Merlin and the pale witch's head also snapped toward the siblings' hiding place. The pale witch smiled, while Merlin's aura turned crimson along the edges once more.

Fury.

He's mad that we've been spying on him, not once, but twice, thought Emrysa.

"Pssst," Dermot hissed nodding his head toward their dwelling. "Come on, quick, let's get out of here before they change their minds and kill us both on the spot."

But Emrysa shook her head. And compelled and repulsed both, Emrysa brought her hands together and called aloud *Patere*—expose.

The wooden slats shimmered around them in an overwhelming heat, then slowly, the edges began to smolder and smoke. Orange embers, bright in the darkness, flickered to life at the center of the circular shape, spreading outwards, exposing Merlin and the pale witch inside, Emrysa and her statuesque brother outside.

Merlin's aura pulsed ruby as he stared in disbelief at Emrysa—her hands still clasped together, smoke spiraling from her fingertips.

The pale witch twitched a half-smile. It looked more like a snarl. "You've been spying on us."

Emrysa shook her hands free from smoke, rubbed her soot-stained palms on her midnight sky dress and stepped through the gap in the barn wall. "This is *our* home. We go where we like, it is you sneaking around behind our backs."

"And you are?" the pale witch enquired coolly, eyeing

Emrysa from head to toe and back again. For half a second, the pale witch's eyes darted to Merlin's glowing aura before returning her cool stare.

"I," Emrysa began, "am your biggest nightmare, you conniving, prissy little bitch. Now, are you going to tell us just how and *why* you plan to kill my brother, or am I —" she brought her hands together to hold a coalescing fire ball, "—going to have to kill you first?"

A wicked smile crept on Emrysa's lips. After all, Hell hath no fury like an overprotective older sister.

A MILLION SUNS

*A*s quick as Emrysa formed her magic, so too did the pale witch; cool lilac light forming from each of her fingertips like purple flames.

"Cease and desist." Merlin scowled, stepping forward and separating them. The two black horses shied from his tone, one with a whicker, kicking up golden straw as it did. Merlin's brow furrowed as he looked from one witch to the other, his eyes lingering longer on Emrysa than perhaps they should.

Dermot managed to lift his jaw from the ground and stepped through the gap in the barn wall. He pulled his sister aside with a nervous half laugh. "You must excuse my cantankerous sister, she's a little protective and a lot boar-headed, and well..." He forced a smile, though Emrysa could feel his hands tremble upon her shoulders. "It's not as if you were having a polite conversation about me, and the thing is—"

"Shut up, Dermot. You're rambling," Emrysa said under her breath.

They all stared at one another. Four young witches caught in an ancient agreement made by the Alchive Council centuries before.

It was the pale witch who spoke first. "So, you are this century's dragon heart?"

"I haven't the foggiest." Dermot laughed with rising nerves.

Emrysa stepped forward. "Cut the riddles, *prettiness*. It's answers we want, not questions."

The pale witch smiled in a way that was not pretty at all. "I doubt your disparaging tone was intended as a compliment. Firstly, my name is not prettiness, but Nimue. And secondly, the only riddle here is your brother, it would seem."

Emrysa felt a probing of her mind; the nosey bitch was rummaging around in her thoughts, her brother's too, she expected. But Emrysa let her continue, after all, she had nothing to hide, and if this Nimue discovered exactly how much Emrysa despised her, how something about her pretty face repulsed her, then all the better.

Nimue scrutinized Emrysa before raising a brow, she turned to Merlin briefly, then, as she read Dermot's thoughts, a flush of red rose to her pale cheeks. She took a moment to compose herself, her steely expression returning once more. "It is true, you have not been fore-warned and neither of you are learned in the matter, which is quite... *unusual.*"

"Not as unusual as your face," Emrysa retorted, amusing herself, and raising a smile on Merlin's lips that transformed his serious face entirely. They shared a conspiratorial glance while her brother scoffed beside her.

"You are petty and pathetic," Nimue said with a resigned sigh.

"Two of my finer traits," Emrysa shot back. "And now that you've violated my mind for your answers, it's time you gave us yours. What the hell *is* a dragon heart and why the hell do you plan to have my brother killed?"

Dermot squeaked beside her while Merlin sucked a short, sharp breath between teeth.

And Nimue smiled her pretty awful smile. "Because, you self-righteous halfway witch, dragons are vermin and must be killed before they kill us."

Dermot jolted and danced between the girls before they began sparring with more than words. He laughed. It wasn't a real laugh. "Ladies, ladies. Let's stop. Just..." he took an exaggerated slow breath. "Everyone just calm down."

"Calm down?!" Now Emrysa strode ahead of Dermot, standing between her brother and the witch Nimue. She held her arms wide as if to protect him. "We can't just let them turn up here with these accusations." She glared at the pale witch. "You can't say these things, threaten these things, look at him for the Goddess's sake!"

And they did. All eyes on Dermot, youngest brother. Lithe and light-hearted. Nervous and void of any magical prowess.

"The problem with you, Emrysa—*one* of your problems—is that you are too busy looking into the minds of people to notice the heart of the matter."

With that, Nimue flicked her fingers at Dermot, who gasped, staggering back several steps. He almost tripped as his feet tangled in the straw, causing the horses to spook and snort once more. He held his heart space, staring into the gleaming glow emanating through the cracks of his fingers. It lit his features, illuminating the worried contours of his face.

"By the Goddess's name, what are you doing?" Emrysa bawled.

"Stop her!" Nimue ordered before Emrysa could bring the spell to her mind and fingertips. Strong hands pulled the crook of her elbows, yanking her body into the stronghold of Merlin's embrace.

"Get off me," Emrysa yelled, watching as the glow at her brother's chest became brighter, radiating from his heart, shimmering until his entire upper torso shone—until the entire barn shone.

"Dermot!" Emrysa yelled, feeling a pull at her own magic, a magnetic force dragging it away from her body and mind. She writhed in Merlin's hold, but it was relentless, overpowering and she could do nothing, *nothing*, to protect her brother from whatever the pale witch, Nimue, had planned. "What are you doing to him? Stop! Get off!"

Merlin's hold only intensified as she squirmed and fought. The magnetic pull amplified. Nimue ignored everything but Dermot, and she cocked her head, trying to read him—his heart space.

"Drop your hands, Dermot," Nimue ordered.

And he did, amazed and dumbfounded and confused.

"Stop this spell!" screamed Emrysa. "Stop it at once you..." she trailed off.

The glow in Dermot's chest faded, as did the look of resolve on Nimue's face. Merlin dropped his hands, Emrysa's magic returning to her body with such force, she fell forward to her knees.

Nimue's pale eyes twitched.

"It wasn't there," Merlin said. "The dragon heart, it was not there... in his chest."

Beside him, Dermot patted his chest like he was trying to put out a fire, while Emrysa scrambled to her feet.

When she rose, she screamed between clenched teeth and shunted Merlin in the chest, wild with anger and frustration both. She could have used magic, but she was too enraged. "Don't you—" Another shunt sent him backwards, "—ever —" A bigger shunt, causing him to trip to the ground. Horses shied and nickered, "— *ever* do that spell on me again! *Ever!*"

Emrysa spun and in two strides was at her brother's side, her hand placed at his heart. And as if there was no-one there to witness the softening of her edges, her voice dropped, her eyes, deep and dark, filled with concern. "Are you okay? Did they hurt you?" she asked. Dermot shook his head, avoiding her gaze. Shaken. It made Emrysa's blood boil.

"Perhaps it is a little early for the beast to stir," Nimue said behind her.

Rage flared in Emrysa, her skin and bones containing an emotion that needed only to escape. "Early? You magnificent half-wit." Emrysa flung her arms outwards; glowing white orbs formed in her hands lighting the shadowed barn. She raised them higher, glowing like a goddess. "You've seen it for yourself, he hasn't got this so-called dragon heart. Now you've checked. You are free to leave. Go on. Off you go! Back to your prissy little Council like the good little sheep you are."

"It doesn't work like that," Nimue said but Emrysa could not stop the rage cascading from her lips like lava.

"What doesn't work like what, you iconic thickhead? Do you even know? Do you know anything for yourself, or do you just believe what you are told?" Emrysa flung her arms with theatrical flair, doing her best to imitate Nimue's voice with an added childish lilt. "This is what they tell me. So this is what I do." She broke character, her venom returning once more, a cold steely venom that was far harsher than any raised words could be. Emrysa enunciated each word with acute precision as she stalked toward the pale witch. "You are not welcome here."

She was but inches away from Nimue, their faces so close they shared breath. Nimue did not flinch. But she did smile, a cold cruel smile that crawled across her lips like spiders hatching from their eggs.

"To threaten a member of the Council is to threaten the Council itself," she said, a glint in her eye that looked like war.

Emrysa raised a thin eyebrow in counterattack. "I

promise you, it is no threat. So you can go and tell *the Council* to piss off."

"Emrysa!" Dermot yelled, her stupidity shaking himself out of his own. He laughed, that tinny hollow sound of fear, while attempting to pull her away at the shoulder. "She doesn't mean it, of course. Ha! What fun!"

It was so typical of Dermot to try to make light, to try to joke and humor his way out of trouble. But he wasn't fooling anybody. Least of all Emrysa. She sent a soothing spell to him, despite her anger and malice. All she wanted was to keep her younger brother safe. Safe and happy.

Safe and happy—and alive.

"It is possible," Merlin began. A life-raft. He cleared his throat when Nimue shot him a death-glare. "It is possible that his heart will not turn."

If he wanted attention, he got it. Even the horses stopped chomping on hay.

"It's something I read once, somewhere..." Merlin almost looked as nervous and out of place as Dermot. "An ancient text that seemed to indicate a dragon heart could miss a generation if the witch in particular was weak of magic—"

"Merlin," Nimue warned, "we've talked about this. Stop."

"I'm only repeating what I have read—"

"It goes against Council's laws, Merlin, *please.*"

At this Emrysa noticed Nimue pulsing out her aura to Merlin's once more. She watched, wondering if Nimue was soothing or... *manipulating* him. Merlin's features hardened once more, his silence returning with the purple aura melding to his own.

Dermot took the silence to take the stage. "My magic is not weak," he protested, and Emrysa groaned, wishing he would just shut up while they had the upper hand. "You lot might throw your magic around all willy-nilly but my magic," he grew in stature and in that moment Emrysa saw the strong man he would grow into... if only she could save him from his lingering fate. "But my magic has a science behind it."

Nimue scoffed, Dermot continued, "It is a thing of beauty, a thing of science and purposeful equations— truth, not manipulation..."

Dermot continued, so nobody noticed the wry smile upon Nimue's face, the lilac light forming at her fingertips. She took one sly sideways glance to Emrysa, then cast.

And the light from Emrysa's chest exploded like a million suns.

6

EXPOSED

*T*he spell sliced across her skin, exposing her heart, glowing like lightning captured in a jar. She didn't feel the pain, not at first, just as blood can seep from a wound inflicted by the sharpest of knives before the mind can process the slash. But instead of blood flowing, it was light and power and magic.

And something else.

Emrysa gasped, her fingers covering the gaping wound that exposed her heart. The light reflected from the faces that stared back at her in awe. The horses shied away with panicked shrieks, their black coats trembling under the strange light as they quivered in the far corner of the barn.

Nimue's face lit up with something other than light.

Something akin to spite and malice and a self-gratifying smile of triumph.

Emrysa looked down at her shining torso, both horrified and mesmerized. Her temples pulsed, beads of cold sweat formed and trailed her cheeks.

Between her ribcages, beneath her skin, a dragon coiled and writhed in the place of Emrysa's heart. Her hands shot to cover her heart-space—a dismal attempt to conceal the beast in a protective embrace. Eyes wide, she found Merlin's gaze, and a vulnerability she had never before experienced tore through her veins—her heart, her body, her *soul*.

Exposed for all to see.

Then she found her brother and despite the turbulence held within the vessel of her mind, she smiled.

He was safe.

Even if she wasn't, her brother was safe.

The knowledge gave her power, strength, and she found her senses once more. With fingers curled like claws, she cast, drawing her skin back over her exposed heart-space, sealing the wound. Sealing her fate.

Emrysa lifted her chin, and an eyebrow, and cast a steely glare to the smirking Nimue.

"Three moons, Emrysa." Nimue smiled her beautiful and terrible smile. "Three moons."

She turned, pushing her aura toward Merlin, whose

dumbfounded face turned soft once more with the touch of her lilac light defusing his own. Whatever words he intended went unsaid as he followed the pale witch from the hole in the barn wall and walked out into the night where the darkness devoured them completely.

There was a long, lingering silence, before Dermot and Emrysa turned to each other, dumbfounded.

"Well..." Dermot began.

"Well..." Emrysa repeated with a loaded pause. "Well... *shit!*"

And though neither could say why, smiles crept across their lips, they shook their heads, and erupted into fits of astonished laughter that trailed out into the cold night-time shadows.

7

SOUL BOND

*E*mrysa's fist stopped just inches from her parents' door. She held it there, mid-knock, as muffled conversation from inside their chamber roused her curiosity and awakened her stealth mode. She placed the finger to her lips, silencing her brother beside her.

"We send her away. First light," Father said, a grave emotionless tone.

"But won't they suspect?" Mother asked, jittery.

"Why should they? The Council believe Dermot to be the last born, they'll never think the dragon heart belongs to her."

Emrysa leant her ear closer to the door, afraid to cast a hearing spell in case she alerted her parents to her

presence. Dermot, taller, listened above her, cupping his
hand between door and ear. Emrysa strained to listen
harder, pressing her entire face against the thick wood
as if that would help her cause. There was a long pause
in the room. Emrysa pressed harder. The door suddenly
swung open and both Emrysa and Dermot tumbled
through, all but falling at Father's feet. Dermot coughed
and regained his composure quickly while Emrysa tried
to hide her amusement. She straightened, smoothing
her dress as a way of distraction, and avoided eye
contact at all cost. She could hear Dermot's suppressed
laugh in the raggedness of his breath, and blurted out a
short, sharp laugh of her own.

"Damn you, child. Why must you always be where
you are not supposed to?" Father growled.

Emrysa shrugged.

"Sorry, Father," Dermot said.

But it was Emrysa's apology Lord Cheval wanted.
And she refused. After all, it was her parents who owed
her the apology. "You're wrong," Emrysa said, when her
anger and frustration muted her humor of the door fail.
"About them not knowing. They know. We know. *I*
know."

A heavy silence lingered, and Emrysa waited, daring
her father to chastise her insolence. He didn't, he just

stared, his ice blue eyes welling with a brewing storm. Mother did not move, she sat, frozen, staring at Emrysa as if she were a precious or terrifying gift.

"They exposed my dragon heart and they've given me three moons," Emrysa said coolly.

Father rushed to her, taking her hands in his and squeezing them with so much force, Emrysa winced. "We won't let them take you," he promised. "We will send you away, like we planned. First light."

"But the Council know. They won't just let me go. They'll hunt me down." Emrysa wished her father would stop squeezing her hands so, but she was too defiant to let him know it hurt. "I need to rid myself of the beast inside—"

"No!" Father yelled. He almost threw her hands away. "No, your beast is part of your soul. Lose that, you may as well let them kill you now."

Mother whimpered. Dermot cast a pained stare.

Emrysa squared her shoulders. "It's your fault, you know. Hiding this from us." Emrysa paced after her father. "All this time we could have made a plan—"

"We had a plan! We lied in the register, we allowed the Council to believe you were the first born, not the last. They were supposed to suspect Dermot and then leave when he didn't turn."

"They were planning on slaughtering him *before* he turned."

"How was I to know?" Father yelled, his face red with rage and fear—spittle forming at the corners of his mouth. "I could only go on what they did to my brother, and my aunt."

Emrysa stepped back, nausea forming in the pit of her stomach. "This knowledge belonged to *me*. You should have told *me* what this family line meant. Not wait and spring it on me unprepared when it happens."

Father shook his head. "You've been prepared for your turn your entire life. Just like my youngest brother. You know who you are. I've never known anyone with so much self-assurance. So much truth to their bones."

"And I've never known someone with so much deception in theirs." The words seemed to punch her father in the solar plexus. "You lied to me my entire life."

"Darling." Mother rose from her chair. "We were trying to protect you."

"And how do you propose to protect me now? By making me flee forever?"

"That's not fair, darling."

"No, no it's not. And that's why I'm going to rid myself of this, this *thing*. I could have had nearly eighteen years to work this out. Now I have three moons."

"I told you before, you are better off dead than trying to sever your soul bond." Father, despite his rage, began to shake with tears. "My girl. Even you, with all your strength and bravery, are not strong enough to live without your soul. Please. Please listen to us. We have a place for you. A safe place where they will not find you. Trust us."

"How can I trust the people who have lied to me my entire life?" Emrysa turned on her heel and stormed away. She feared if she spoke again, she would cry; she would not let her parents see her so weak. Not now, not when she needed all the strength she could muster.

"Wait," Dermot called, jogging to catch up.

"Gather your belongings," Mother called after her. "We'll make a plan. You'll leave at first light."

Staring straight ahead as they walked from their parents' chamber, Emrysa spoke to Dermot. "Magic has laws," she said. Dermot said nothing. He already had an idea where this was going. "But alchemy does not abide by these same laws, is that right?"

"You're right. There is a—"

"Science. Yes, yes. As you keep saying. And this wormhole you mentioned earlier?" Emrysa let the question dangle, she could almost hear Dermot's mind ticking. "Do you think it can contain a dragon?"

"Sister, I do not know. But there is only one way to find out."

They broke into a jog, and then sprinted toward the alchemy chamber.

They did not notice Merlin hiding within the shadows.

8

A RUSH OF BLOOD

*E*mrysa and Dermot skittered around corners and corridors, retracing the same steps they had run in fits of laughter only hours earlier. Now, night seeped through the windows, casting them in shadows between newly lit sconces high upon the wall.

They burst through the alchemy chamber and Emrysa stopped in her tracks.

"Shit!" she cursed, taking in the destruction of the make-shift laboratory. "What in the Goddess's name happened in here?"

All around smashed vials spewed out dangerous looking smoke, from them, a repugnant smell caused Emrysa to cover her nose as she breathed short, shallow breaths. Next to her, Dermot stood agog, taking in the chaos with a pained expression.

"Do you think *they* did it?" Dermot asked.

Emrysa didn't answer as she paced a circle, careful not to step on the broken glass as she did. "It makes no sense for the Council to smash this place up. What would they gain from it?"

Dermot sighed long and hard. "I'm going to fetch Rhian to help clean up this mess. I can't concentrate or work with all this chaos around me."

He slipped out, calling Rhian's name. Emrysa smiled —he always did have a thing for the young maid.

Behind her, the door creaked open.

Merlin crept through taking unsure and apologetic steps as if waiting for Emrysa's consent. She watched him. Without the pale witch close, his features wore a tired expression, as if a mask of lies and light-heartedness had been lifted from his face, along with her violet aura.

"What do you want?" Emrysa barked, though a strange magnetic force pulled her closer to him.

Merlin hesitated. "To help."

"To help kill me?" She crossed her arms over her chest, though her heart had already been exposed.

"No, I wish to help *you*." He stalked cautiously forward, and Emrysa found herself holding her breath. She noticed, now he was closer, the faint freckles across the bridge of his nose and cheeks. The upward curl of his eyelashes framing his hypnotic hazel eyes. But still, she couldn't allow herself to trust him.

"Why?"

Merlin shook his head. "I don't rightly know. At first, I agreed to this enlisting because I have a deep fascination with dragon lore and the myths and legends surrounding dragon hearts. Now, I seem to have a deeper fascination with you. You feel it too. I know you do. In the eaves, when I first saw you, that was the moment."

Emrysa scoffed and turned away, trying to ignore her fluttering heart. "The moment for what?"

"The moment I realized I would do anything for you."

Emrysa thought back to his ruby-red aura when he found her spying on her. *No, not raging,* Emrysa thought. *Lust, passion.* She gulped, trying to dampen the flame rising in her blood.

"I doubt Nimue will be happy to hear you say that."

"I doubt anything would make Nimue happy—except of course, power. It's the only thing she wants," Merlin said.

"It's not the *only* thing." Emrysa raised her eyebrows suggestively and it was Merlin's turn to scoff.

"You are talking about her aura's influence over me." Merlin smiled the type of smile Emrysa knew could break her heart. "She doesn't think I know. I only allow her to do it because it allows a connection for me to understand her, to listen to her thoughts. I find I am safer that way."

"You don't trust the prissy little wench, either?"

Merlin laughed. "I don't trust her. I don't trust the Council. And they don't know who I am. Not really. They don't understand my power. I'm there only to gather intelligence."

Emrysa would have asked for who, but he was so close now, she could see the shades of gold in his irises, and the pull of nature grabbed her heart. Like magnets, they were drawn closer. Merlin took a strand of Emrysa's raven hair in his fingers, the light tingle of the pull sending shivers up her spine. She couldn't understand it, but Emrysa felt a desperate desire to taste his lips, to feel his kiss. His hand cradled the back of her head now and pulled her face to his own—not that she needed the guidance. Her lips parted. Her breath short. Her beast stirred within her heart, bounding and dancing against the cavity in her chest. His lips found her own, like lightning finding ground. The shock reeled in her mind but her body could not let go.

Then it happened.

The rush of blood over skin, a heat too hot to bear. Merlin pulled away, his lips, his fingertips blistering. His eyes wide in terror. And she didn't need to ask why. She could she see her reflection in his eyes. She could see the scales ripple over the skin of her arms.

She could feel her dragon heart awaken.

Confused. Distraught, Emrysa tried to call out, but in the place of her scream, angry golden flames erupted from her mouth just as Nimue darted through the doorway.

In her hands, the pale witch wielded a broadsword. She spun it hand over wrist and it sliced the air with her cruel laugh. Nimue clutched the sword, staring deeply into Emrysa's eyes, and raised it behind her shoulder.

She wasn't going to wait to slay the dragon.

9

FALLING

*E*mrysa bellowed—the force of her call sending both Merlin and Nimue crashing to the ground. The golden sword fell from Nimue's hand, skittering across the flagstones. More vials smashed. Windows cracked. The very ground trembled.

But Emrysa continued to roar with the spell she pulled from the deepest part of herself—a soul-severing spell. She had no other choice.

She staggered backward, seeing her reflection in the cracked windows. It wasn't the scales rippling over her own body that repulsed Emrysa as the spell began to form, but the way her body jolted and contorted into impossible shapes. She yelled in pain, the sound grating against her aching bones.

Something inside her recoiled, hid, burrowed down

deep not wanting to be touched. The dragon? Her soul?
Her conscience, perhaps. *Her grace?* But deeper she dug,
pulling at the threads of her fraying soul until she grappled it with her mind completely.

She would not let the pale witch take her. She would
not allow Nimue the satisfaction of plunging the golden
sword into her flesh.

So in her mind, Emrysa whispered the words
through short, sharp gasps of pain.

"I use my soul to save my heart
To make the beast within depart.
Split my spirit, sever the ties
Release my soul out to the skies."

The spell. It felt like taking a huge breath just before
diving into freezing water. You know what's coming,
you know it's going to hurt. Your body goes tight, taut,
your heart clenches, and then, you jump...

THE FALL WAS long and lonely and dark. An empty space
in which Emrysa plummeted, smashing through memories and experiences and savored moments. And as she
crashed through, each memory spoiled, like a stone
thrown into a peaceful lake, the calm surface shattered
and perfect reflections distorted. Everything she knew
was breaking until there was nothing but black.

And from there, she heard it.

The voice.

Would you really let me go?

She knew it to be her soul. And in the moment, all she wished was to hold it, embrace it, keep it safe inside her body. But somewhere, in the stillness and silence, she could make out the rhythm of her dragon heart and she knew what she had to do.

Yes, Emrysa said. *I shall let a* part *of you go.*

And with that permission, a rip sliced across her entire being. A cut. A wound as painful as lost love and heartbreak. A searing agony so cold it burnt, while white hot air hurt her lungs to breathe. She swam upwards from the darkness, upwards from the pit of her being. Upwards to the distant screams and shouts coming from the light.

Nearly there. Her fingers breached the surface. Her life force returned in a *whoosh*, like a long, hard inhale. Suddenly, Emrysa was back. She returned to her body with a gasp. And although she was no longer submerged in her subconsciousness, Emrysa felt like she was drowning all the same.

A piece—a large piece—of her had gone. And despite the room coming into focus; Merlin's calls and Nimue's screams, her brother staring with horrified howls, Emrysa had never felt so empty, so alone. So... *lonely.*

The world around her seemed to hover in slow motion, faded and muted.

From the corner of her eye, Dermot ran to her, scrambling on his hands and knees to hold her. Emrysa's seizures finished, her face calm as she gathered her breath with the new emptiness residing within. But she was safe. She was alive, and she knew loneliness was a price she would have to be happy to pay to see another day.

Merlin was at her side now; his lips were moving but she could not hear his words. She focused on the shape of his lips, the movement of his tongue. The urgency in his eyes. Then the ringing quietened, and she began to hear him. A whisper at first before his rages deafened.

"Emrysa!" Merlin yelled. "Emrysa, can you hear me?"

Both he and Dermot stared at her chest and Emrysa found herself too scared to follow their gaze. What had the spell done? What caused their faces to grimace so?

A glow formed, golden and bright, lighting up their faces and glinting on the sword's sleek blade on the ground. The glow was coming from her. From her heart space. A dreadful thought crept through her veins.

Had she incanted the soul spell in vain?

There were so many questions she wanted to ask, but the glow from her chest erupted, blinding her. Blinding everyone. Dermot fell to the ground. Emrysa and Merlin covered their eyes with the crook of their elbows, and from Emrysa's heart space, the dragon emerged.

It pushed and pulled its way out of her, its size unfathomable as it continued to shriek and roar and writhe. Emrysa watched on, horrified and silent as the beast burst from her chest in a golden haze. She slumped to the ground with exhaustion when it finally tore free from her.

She turned to Dermot, holding her chest. She had done it—the impossible. A quick smile was all she could afford.

The dragon flew and coiled through the room, angered at its separation. It was not fully formed, more like the spirit of itself—ghostly pale and almost translucent. Yet it still clattered into things, causing mayhem in the lab, and Emrysa, for once, had no idea what to do. She watched with a mixture of longing and pity and a terrible sense of loss, knowing a part of her very being had been stripped from her body.

It continued, not angered, but confused. Scared. Mirroring Emrysa's own sense of tragic mourning. The beast called into the night-time air. A mournful wail of loss and emptiness. As it did, a wail broke from Emrysa. A guttural howl grating on bone and sinew. She staggered from hands and knees, swaying when she finally stood. Merlin grabbed her when she stumbled, supporting her as she tried to gather strength. But watching the beast wail and thrash, she wondered if she would ever know true strength again.

"Freeze the damned thing!" Nimue screamed, and without waiting, she cast her spell of ice that clung to the beast's body, immobilizing it as it hung in the space above their heads. "It will at least give us time to work out what to do."

Nimue scowled at Emrysa, but Emrysa had neither fight nor care to rise to her bait.

Beneath the beast frozen above their heads in mid-flight, the witches stared with a mixture of awe and revulsion. Merlin's eyes followed the contours of its body, spellbound by its beauty, its regality that had emanated from Emrysa since the first time he had set eyes on her. Dermot watched on with a mixture of pity and concern, his eyes dancing back and forth from beast to sibling. Nimue watched with glee, and something else not easy to discern.

Emrysa simply watched with tear stained cheeks and gasping breath. The dragon's eye suddenly rolled, ice dripping like tears. It focused on Emrysa and whimpered a mournful song once more.

"It won't work long, look," said Nimue, pointing.

The ice continued to melt, sizzling upon hot scales before dripping to the ground.

One more second and it was on the move again, this time heading straight toward Emrysa. The impact smashed into her chest, sending her flying to crash on her back at the far side of the chamber.

"Emrysa!" Dermot yelled, watching as the beast pushed helplessly against his sister.

"It's trying to get back into her body," Merlin yelled, his tone laced with sadness and pity.

It's trying to get back into my heart, Emrysa thought, feeling the loss, needing to feel the dragon back inside as much as it wished to return.

But it was impossible, the spell had banished it from its host's body, and so it pounded against her, its ghost-like form finding purchase each time. Emrysa yelled out with pain and heartbreak with each fail. She heard her own ribs crack with the dragon's force. But her howl came from a deeper place than physical pain, a darker place. A place of hopelessness.

Like a poem half formed, Emrysa tried to pull at a spell, to find the right words, the right sentiment, the right *belief* to reverse the soul spell. To imbue the dragon spirit once more. *I would rather live a short life whole than a whole life empty,* she thought wistfully. Nearly there, she could feel the forming of the right words on her tongue.

A sonic boom erupted from the chamber. But it didn't come from her spell. It came from somewhere else. It came from... Dermot.

He held one hand aloft palm flat out ahead of him. His other hand circled with a gathering speed. And from his hand, a darkness came. An emptiness. A hole. A place between time and space, spiraling with stars and nebula, moons and comets.

It was truly mesmerizing.

The dragon spirit must have thought so too, as it turned tail, and charged toward the portal.

SMOKE AND STARS

"*N*o, no, *no!*" Emrysa screamed as the dragon sailed through.

She felt the separation growing, the loneliness intensifying. She needed her spirit back, she needed to feel her heart pound with the rhythmical roar she had never been aware of until its loss. In fear, she found her strength and darted after the beast.

"Emrysa, *no!*" Dermot yelled, grabbing her hand and pulling her back. "I have no idea where this portal leads. You can't just go in! We might not ever get you back."

"I don't care," Emrysa cried. "I need to get it back. I have to reverse the spell."

"You stupid girl," Nimue scowled. "You achieve this amazing feat—ensured your safety, changed the course of the dragon heart slaying for future generations—and you want to go and *reverse the spell?*"

Emrysa turned to the pale witch, her dark eyes full of sadness. When she spoke, her tone was tinged with tragedy. "I can't be without it." She turned to the portal whirling glittering smoke and stars. Hypnotized, she walked toward it.

"Shut the thing down!" Nimue yelled to Dermot. But his face was red, his hands shook, his veins pulsed at his temples.

"I cannot!" Dermot yelled back. Yet closer Emrysa walked. "I cannot stop it. It will not leave my hands. It's pulling at my life force. If I stop, I fear it will take me with it."

Emrysa wished to run, to charge through after her dragon soul but the spell had rendered her weak. Each step felt mired in quicksand.

Nimue raised her hands, casting them to Dermot; pale lilac crackled toward him. "I'll try to sever the bond. Merlin, for the Goddess's sake, *do something!* Don't let her go in."

But Merlin was frozen to the spot, watching through shock or something else.

"It's working!" Dermot called, feeling the connection falter. "The portal is going to close."

But his celebration was short lived... Emrysa had

stepped one foot closer to the portal. She knew she was close. She knew she was almost there as long as...

"Wait!" Merlin yelled, breaking suddenly from his reverie. He raced to Emrysa as she took her first step through. He dove, grabbing for her hand. Their fingers touched. She turned, her face etched with sorrow. "Emrysa, wait. We can work this out."

But she shook her head, mouthed sorry, and disappeared into the darkness.

11

THE FOREST BLACK

*T*here was a chaotic whirling of space and time. Stars imploding, comets racing. Worlds forming. Then, nothing. Just the sound of blood pumping through veins, and the shoreline sound of breath leaving lungs.

Darkness, utter darkness, had a sound. A heavier sound than silence. A suppressive ache behind eyes and over ears. A void that fit the exact shape of Emrysa and held her in its fierce clutches.

It lasted a moment and a lifetime. Four blind paces forward. An intake of breath. Hands reaching, floundering.

Then a snap as a branch broken under foot cracked the silence open. Emrysa blinked as her surroundings came into view. She lowered her hands.

Where am I?

A night-time wood surrounded her. Thick and dense and all but dead. No leaves grew on these branches. No grass underfoot. Just the smell of death and decay and a sinister breeze that wrapped its way around her limbs. She looked for the dragon spirit but it was nowhere to be seen in the blackened sky. She couldn't *feel* it. Wherever her dragon heart had gone, it had not gone to this realm. For the briefest of moments, she was momentarily awed by her brother's science. It was indeed a form of magic.

"A multi-dimensional portal?" Emrysa considered aloud. Her voice broke the stifling silence. Then followed the slither and creaking of branches blowing on the wind. No, not blowing, reaching. Reaching for her. She backed away, but poisoned vines continued to inch their way toward her, creaking and groaning as they did—wrapping themselves around her ankles while heavy thorn-laden branches bowed down, grasping.

She flicked a hand to cast the strange branches away, and they did so with a shrill scream. But nothing else stirred in the woods. No birds flocked away from the sound. No crickets or beasts. Frantic, Emrysa continued casting away the vines trailing up to her knees now. She placed a hand on the weathered bark of a tree to steady herself as she wriggled her leg free, but the bark under her hand moved at her touch.

She pulled away, looking at the tree then her hand gooey with a slick, tepid liquid. Emrysa gasped, her palm was covered in black, but there was something else, something worse than the stench of death on her hand. Etched in the tree bark, where her hand had once been, was a face, twisted and contorted in a tortured, silent scream.

She should move away, she knew she should. Run. Flee. But she didn't. Curious with morbid fascination, Emrysa stepped forward, inching her face toward the bark.

So slowly she couldn't tell if it was really happening or a figment of her imagination, the eyes within the tortured tree-face rolled toward her, groaning like a rotten floorboard as they did.

She gasped.

It moved again, quicker this time, another painful and agonized silent scream, as if the face wished to make itself heard now it had an audience.

"What is this place?" she questioned, backing up, spinning. Gasping.

Now her eyes had grown accustomed to the gloom, she could see the horror of this place. Every tree had a face formed in its bark, each one a picture of terror. Like snapshots shuttering in and out of focus, she saw them. One, two, ten, a hundred. Creaking began again, the slow, insidious reach of dark branches and vines. She spun, breathless, but something else caught her eye, stopping Emrysa from fighting off the clutching vines.

Blackness. A solid mass of blackness surging angrily into itself, hovering about the ground.

The dark force hurtled toward her. It had no shape, just a mass of black and a terrible feeling of dread. It swirled with a thrumming noise laced with threats, getting louder as it raced forward.

She had no time to think. She had no time to run. She had nowhere *to* run. But on the blackness hurtled, screaming now, piercing her ears, ripping deep at her bone marrow. It pulled at her fraying soul. And then another pull, a yank.

A hand on her hand.

Darkness. Nothingness. Silence. Then the light and sounds of her own world flooded back and over-whelmed her.

Emrysa fell as she was sucked out of the portal with an audible pop. Not onto ground, but onto Merlin who groaned beneath the force of her fall.

"Oh, thank the fickle and menacing Goddess of luck! We got you back." Dermot offered her his hand. "We thought we'd lost you."

Clumsily, she rose, accidentally pressing one hand against Merlin's nether regions as she pushed herself up, causing him to groan all the more. Dermot could hardly contain his excitement. He had been working on his wormhole for as long as Emrysa could remember. He had never achieved a full portal opening. Nothing had never gone through... and certainly nobody had ever come back out.

"We made a sort of human chain to pull you out but..." Dermot trailed off, noticing the haunted look in Emrysa's once vibrant eyes. "What happened? In there? Where were you?"

"Where's the dragon?" Nimue asked.

But Emrysa shook her head. Silent. Even if she wanted to answer the bombardment of questions, she could not. What happened in there could not be summed up with words, and she didn't *ever* want to think about where she had been and that unrelenting force that hurtled toward her. She staggered, finding the need to sit before her legs gave way under the weight of her experience.

She grabbed a chair, flicking off the broken glass and the remnants from the beast's chaos with her hands, *too tired to spell cast.* She sat with a *humph*, then, gaining some small amount of composure, looked up to her brother.

"Are *you* okay?" she asked.

"*Me*? I am absolutely dandy, you raving plonker. You on the other hand, look like a disheveled scullery maid —" he turned to the wide-eyed, wild-haired maid in the room. "No offence, Rhian."

By the way the maid's red cheeks flushed with breathless wonder, Emrysa knew Rhian must have joined in the human chain to help pull her back into their world. She gave Rhian a wan smile, who returned the gesture with her characteristic awe.

"Blimmin' heck, Miss, if that weren't blimmin' exciting!" She smiled, exposing a charming gap between her front two teeth. The freckles upon her nose stretched across the canvas of her face with the width of her smile.

Emrysa could not help but to smile back. "Thank you for your help, Rhian. As always, I am indebted to you," Emrysa said, and they both held a gaze full of unspoken secrets. Had anyone been paying close attention, perhaps they would have noticed. But thankfully, the events had turned everybody's mind to other things.

"Your dragon heart is gone, but where *is* your dragon?" Nimue pressed and Emrysa sighed. At least the prissy bitch didn't seem to want to kill her anymore, but that didn't take away the sting—because of the pale witch, Emrysa feared she would never again feel whole again. She would always be a shell, her soul untethered.

Alone. Or worse—she thought of the terrors she discovered in the other realm—not alone.

"No more questions," Merlin said tenderly. He pressed a hand to her forehead, and she closed her tired eyes. "You're burning up. You should get some rest. The questions can wait until the morning, can they not?"

Emrysa groaned in appreciation, and her tiredness was so deep, she could only make out the muffled sound of conversation, but not the words themselves. She just wanted to sleep. To fall into a black hole and be reunited with her soul spirit once more. Perhaps in her dreams, this was possible. It was her brother's voice that came into focus first.

"Come, I'll lead you," said Dermot. "Don't worry, I'll make sure you're asleep before I tell our parents of the events."

Emrysa cringed. "They won't be happy that I've done this."

"The miserable old biddies are never happy, sister. Now, come." Emrysa smiled at Merlin as he moved his hand from her forehead and flashed a warm smile that melted her heavy, empty heart. In a daze, she allowed her brother to lead her away to her chamber.

.   .   .

MERLIN FOLLOWED them from the alchemy chamber, then stopped and watched the Chevals walk gingerly along the corridor, farther and farther away from him. He didn't have the heart to tell Emrysa that a nagging fear remained within his bones. He heard the laboratory door close behind him but didn't look back for Nimue. He could do without her pushing her aura all over him this evening. But they did need to inform the Council that their work here was done. The dragon heart had been dealt with, though no doubt, it would raise even more questions. He turned to make his way to his own chamber, knowing sleep would elude him no matter how exhausted he felt.

Wrapped up in their own thoughts, nobody noticed the tiny spot of the portal behind the lab's closed door had not yet sealed together.

A spot. A dot, nothing more. And nobody noticed the dark, formless mass the color of dread seeping through that tiny gap into their world.

Nobody, except Nimue.

PART II

"To start a rumor, one needs only an element of truth. Ensure one central fact, and no matter how outlandish the lies surrounding it become, they will believe. They believe because the Whole Truth is inconceivable, while lies can be shaped perfectly to fit the mind of the receiver.

The danger in rumors and lies depends on the venom and delicacy of those who fabricate these dangerous tapestries. It helps, also, if the one who starts the rumor has sweet lips, and a sweeter face. And if her venom is aimed at another with *even more* beauty than she, all are likely to agree.

The one thing the world loves-to-love more than a pretty face, is to hate it."

—Emrysa Cheval

12

MIDNIGHT SHADOWS

*E*mrysa found no comfort in her luxurious bed. Sleep eluded her, no matter how heavy her eyelids. Every time she closed them, the tree faces screamed their silent scream and her eyes shot open once more. The memory—the rush of the darkness—clung to her heart and made it pound. The moon was low in the sky, rising late and offering little light through the small window. Only darkness bled its way through, creeping up to her bed, threatening to smother her.

Quiet footsteps made their way toward her chamber door, accompanied by a warm glow filtering through the small gap between door and ground. The footsteps stopped outside. A dark shadow stilled in the low light. Emrysa waited for the knock.

Her parents perhaps, though she hoped not. She no longer had the strength to stand resilient. Her brother more likely, unable to sleep after the day's events like her? *Merlin*, she hoped.

The door creaked open. She held her breath.

It was not who she was expecting.

"What do you want?" Emrysa spat, pulling the covers around her.

Nimue said nothing, just glided forward, small candle held aloft. She didn't ask before perching herself on the end of the bed. Nimue paused, her haughty nose stuck in the air.

"You think you've won by ridding yourself of your dragon heart," Nimue said. Emrysa remained silent. "And I would congratulate you, if it wasn't for the madness you have created."

"Madness?" Emrysa scoffed. "What are you talking about? I have got rid of the thing, so you and your prissy little Council can no longer threaten me. So, yes. I have won." Yet despite her words, Emrysa felt only loss. "You may go now. Go on, off with you!"

Nimue didn't reply immediately, instead, she pulled her pretty face into a thoughtful grimace that made Emrysa want to punch it.

"Do you know where you went? In the portal?" Nimue asked.

"No."

"Hmmm." Nimue paused for a long while and Emrysa found herself disquieted by the silence. Eventually, the pale witch spoke again. "Do you know what you brought back with you?"

"Brought back? I didn't bring anything back, except my family's safety." But Emrysa's mind flitted to those nightmare silent screams etched into blackened bark, the mass of darkness hurtling toward her before Merlin pulled her back into her world.

"Mmmm," Nimue said.

Emrysa sighed with frustration. "If you've come here to tell me something, just come out with it. Your riddles are setting my teeth on edge."

Nimue leant in to Emrysa, eyes burning with such intensity, Emrysa didn't know if the witch would kill or kiss her.

"Close enough," Emrysa said, when Nimue's face was only inches from her own.

The pale witch smiled sickly sweet, then whispered, *"The Darkness is coming."*

For a moment, Emrysa was stunned into silence before a near aggressive laugh erupted from her throat. "The Darkness? *What. Are. You. Talking. About. You. Stupid. Little. Wench?"*

Nimue tossed the candle away, pounding both hands

beside Emrysa's head against the headboard. The
candlelight fizzled out, leaving them caught in shadows
and darkness. Nimue slithered onto the bed, straddling
Emrysa's body. Emrysa tensed but remained still as
Nimue brought her face to her own once more. She felt
the pale witch's warm breath, felt her soft flesh against
her own chest. But still, she did not move.

"You think you're safe by ridding your dragon
heart..." Now Nimue cupped Emrysa's face in her hands.
"But by coming back from that place, not only is your
life at greater risk." Nimue pushed her body harder
against Emrysa, who gasped, breath quivering. "But
you've put *everybody's* lives at risk."

Emrysa's felt her pulse rising, her adrenalin soaring.
She didn't know why; she didn't *want* to know why.
Maybe it was the underlying threat beneath Nimue's
words. Maybe it was something else.

"You conducted a soul spell, didn't you? It is forbid-
den." Then Nimue grabbed Emrysa's face to her own,
parting her lips and thrusting her tongue violently into
Emrysa's mouth. This was nothing of the gentle almost-
kiss with Merlin only hours before—the tender desire of
something beautiful. This kiss was savage storms and
torn hearts. Yet Emrysa allowed Nimue to continue
grabbing at her, pulling at her, ravaging her. Hands and
hair. Breathlessness and heartbeats.

Finally, Emrysa pulled back, "Stop! *Stop.*"

The witches glared at each other in the darkness, chests heaving.

"What are you *doing?*" Emrysa pushed Nimue from her, pushed the desire spell from herself too. "Why would you do that?"

"To give you a chance." Nimue was back to her riddles again.

"Give me a chance of *what?*"

"To be on my side."

Before Emrysa had a chance to bark her refusal, a deafening roar raced along the corridors outside. Louder than a thunderstorm over head. Louder than the tumbling of dreams and nightmares. A soul shaking shriek Emrysa recognized at once.

"Shit!" Emrysa shot up. "It's here! The *thing* is here."

"The Darkness," Nimue said, knowing.

In a flash, Emrysa thought of the dark coalescing mass, the fear it produced, the dread it spread. It was here, in her world, she knew it as sure as her own dragon-less heartbeat.

"We have to warn everyone, quick!" Emrysa grabbed Nimue's hand when the pale witch stood paralyzed to the spot. "Come on. There's nearly a hundred people in the castle's grounds. We need to warn them. We need to warn *everyone.*"

Emrysa had no idea what the Darkness would do, but she knew it would be bad. *Really bad.* She raced to the door, grappling the handle to pull it open. Nothing happened. She rattled the handle harder, the whirling outside getting louder. But the door remained shut, locking her in. She pounded her fists against the heavy dark oak, then gathered a spell to blast the door open. It didn't work, but the boom sent both Emrysa and Nimue flying to the far end of the room.

As they rose, unsteady, the thunderous echoes disappeared along the hallways and corridors as quickly as they came—the silence left in its wake deep and dark. *Unnatural.*

"I hate to say this," Emrysa said, straightening her thin nightdress, "But we're going to need to tell my parents. And they're going to *kill* me."

"Well, it will save the Council a job," Nimue said, raising an eyebrow with the smallest of smiles—not a mean smile. A real smile. Emrysa balked.

"Don't tell me... Did you just... *tell a joke?*"

"Perhaps."

Emrysa shook her head. "Well, will wonders ever cease?" She motioned to the door. "Come on, let's try again."

They both scarpered across the room but before they

got there, heavy footsteps pounded toward them. Several sets of footsteps.

"Emrysa!" yelled Dermot.

The door swung open, and Dermot came to an abrupt halt, his face etched in agony. "Emrysa, come quick, I've found Mother and Father."

His tone, his face, it was all wrong and Emrysa's blood curdled, turning cold and hard. She grabbed his hands. "Where are they?"

"It's not *where* are they, but *what* they are." Dermot paused but his hands made frantic shapes as he tried to formulate the words.

"Spit it out, Dermot, for the Goddess's sake!" Emrysa yelled. "What are they?!"

"They're dead," Dermot yelled back, running his hands through his hair. "They're dead, Emrysa."

13

THE STENCH OF EVIL

She didn't wait for Dermot to explain, she just ran, lightning swift toward their parents' chamber—ignoring the sense of foreboding lingering in the night-time air. Ignoring her brother's plea to wait as he, Merlin and Nimue followed quickly behind.

Where are the guards? There should be guards! But the corridors were empty. No panic. No confusion. No worried maids and servants scuttling around. No Cheval men of arms rallying. Just an eerie silence bar the heaviness of her breath and the beating of her dragon-less heart. She finally reached her parents' chamber door and paused. Upon it, a black mark sparkled like cobalt, singed deep into the thick mahogany wood.

"What is that?" she thought aloud, tracing the mark with her fingertips; two crescent moons back-to-back.

It burned and something deep inside of her yearned. She jumped away.

"What is that?" Dermot repeated between pants as he reached her.

"Step away," ordered Merlin. "It stinks of evil. Nobody touch it, it's insidious."

Emrysa wiped her hand on her nightdress, not wanting to admit she had already touched the mark, hoping she could somehow wipe off its stain.

She braced herself, taking a deep breath, then grabbed the door handle. Dermot placed a hand on her shoulder, pulling her back. She turned to face him, and he shook his head, *no*.

Regardless, she pushed open the door.

The room was cold. More than cold. Bitter and ice and impossibly dark. Shapes and shadows shifted. Emrysa stepped forward, a metallic odor caught in her throat as her bare toes stepped into a warm puddle of...

Dermot grabbed her, pulling his sister back to him once more. "Careful," he urged.

Emrysa lifted her hand to summon fire to her palm to light the way.

In a flash she saw it. Saw *them*—her parents. She stifled a scream, but a whimper escaped. Something else shrieked louder, its breath extinguishing her flame. Darkness prevailed.

Emrysa could hear the short, shallow breaths of her brother, Merlin, and Nimue behind her while she tried to steady her own. Nobody spoke but their fear held its own voice.

Hidden in shadows, Emrysa trembled, and though she wished to never see the gruesome image again, she *had* to. She *had* to find out what happened... and... what was in the room.

With a timid gesture, Emrysa cast a dim light spell. This time the otherworldly shriek was louder, if that was even possible, and immediately, the light was extinguished before she could witness the grisly death of her parents once more. She clasped her hands over her ears as the shrieking pitch hit a crescendo. The noise subsided, but its effect did not. Emrysa turned to her brother. He didn't say a word, but within the shadows she saw his head shake.

Merlin placed a hand on Emrysa's shoulder, and she jumped at his touch. She glanced over at him. "I think I know what this is..." she whispered urgently. "I felt it before—"

"Before, where?" Merlin asked although none of them needed her to answer to know the truth of it.

This, this *thing*, was not of their world. This Darkness, this... hopelessness. It was darker than their world could perceive. And whatever it was, it had killed Lord and Lady Cheval in a way that would stain Emrysa's mind for eternity. Her heart, already heavy, pulled itself deeper into gloom. And she had a terrible feeling that everyone she had ever loved would leave her. Leave her to rot a lonely death.

"This is the madness you brought back with you, Emrysa." Nimue joined her side, sliding in as silent as an assassin.

Deep in the darkness, they could all see it now—the mass had formed together to make a shape, darker than the shadows, snaking and coiling its way ever forward.

"Well, don't just stand there gawping like idiots," Emrysa cursed, pain in her heart from her parent's death escaping as fury. "Let's blast this thing to Kingdom come."

All four dropped to a defensive crouch, palms braced toward the entwining darkness; each with they own powerful spell glowing.

Red. Blue. Green. Purple.

There was no shriek this time as their glows shone enough to light the macabre site once more.

"By the Goddess," Merlin hissed.

Emrysa and Dermot did their best not to look, although Emrysa could see from the corner of her eye.

She could see what she wished she could not. She felt herself heave, then the acrid burn of vomit blazed her throat, her mouth, and she retched onto the floor. Head bowed over her knees she could see exactly what the flagstones were stained with as her vomit hit the ground with a *slop.* Disgust roiled in the pit of her stomach making her heave again.

A scream erupted, transforming into a wail—then began the whirring Emrysa had first heard in the darkened forest. She rose, watching the mass as it writhed and coiled, faster, wilder. It was angered, whatever this was. Angered by their light. By their working together. She prepared herself once more, re-joining the group and braced for attack. It hurtled toward them.

"Now!" Emrysa yelled.

Together, the bright colors charged from their hands, pounding into the Darkness. With a screech, the Dark-ness parted in the exact places of collision, holes the sizes of a fist sizzled and smoked through the mass. The bright colors turned to grey ash, rendering their spells useless.

"Shit!" Emrysa cursed.

"We can't attack it," Merlin yelled over the growing scream of the Darkness.

"Then we need to defend," Emrysa said. "We need to

immobilize it, stop it from leaving this room. Stop it from escaping into the world."

"What we need," Nimue grunted, "is help from the Alchive Council."

This time, Emrysa did not disagree. They needed all the help they could get, and there were none so powerful as the Council.

"Still," Dermot said. "We need to deal with this thing now!"

They thrust their arms outwards, casting their own versions of a protective barrier, but it was no good. The Darkness, like smoke, simply found the gaps, the weak points and morphed its shape to get through any spell they created. But they continued in an avalanche of spell casting. Intricate hand movements, wild arm gestures, incantations, roars and rages. Nothing, *nothing*, worked.

"It is useless," Nimue said without emotion. "There is nothing we can do to stop the Darkness spreading. It is out of our hands. It is out of our control."

With that, the Darkness almost seemed to laugh, a strange sound of serrated edges and jagged blades. Then it bolted with a sudden blink of an eye to Emrysa. It stopped just as suddenly and hovered in the space before her. *Time* seemed to hover before her, as if the world stopped turning.

Frozen to the spot, only her eyes widened, and in a

swift half-second the Darkness morphed, elongating, details forming, until it turned into the shape of Emrysa. A darkened version of herself staring right back at her.

Emrysa stepped back.

The Darkness followed.

Emrysa brought her hand to her mouth to stifle a brewing scream.

The Darkness mimicked her every move, but it did not stifle its scream. Instead, it shrieked its otherworldly call in her face, sending Merlin, Dermot, and Nimue crashing to the gore-covered floor. They clasped their ears, painting blood on their faces from the burgundy puddle soaking the flagstone floor. But just as the Darkness seeped through their spells, the otherworldly yells seeped through their fingers, piercing ear drums and soul.

Only Emrysa remained standing, staring at the darkened version of herself as it yelled in her face. And its sound, its scratching metal-on-metal voice morphed in her blood. She heard it. She could understand it.

It spoke to her.

"You will succumb to me," it said, cold and cruel, a leering and taunting command.

"No!" yelled Emrysa. "I will never succumb to your darkness."

But she felt her fraying soul betray her mind. She

tried to grapple with it, pull its edges, but the more she did, the more it unravelled. *Is this what it means to lose your soul, to lose command of your own desires?*

"You and I are as one," the Darkness continued. *"Come with me..."*

Her blackened form smoked into a shapeless mass once more and in a half-breath, it bolted from the dead Lord and Lady Cheval's bedchamber and hurtled through the door, expanding as it travelled.

Emrysa watched the others scramble to their feet, looking for any sign they may have heard what she had. Sharing a fearful glance at her brother, a longing look of approval from Merlin, and a disdainful half-glance at Nimue, Emrysa spun, gathering her nightdress in her clutches.

"Emrysa, wait!" Dermot yelled. "You can't do this alone. You always try to do everything alone!"

But it was too late, she was already charging after the Darkness, telling herself she was chasing it down, promising herself she was not following its command.

And she prayed with her fraying soul that she was telling herself the truth.

14

BLAME

$\mathcal{U}$nease settled upon Emrysa as she chased the elusive Darkness. It tore through the corridors, expanding as it did until it rounded the first spiral staircase and disappeared. While she could no longer see the shifting mass, she could follow its wake. Every place it touched reeked of death. Mold now appeared, creeping up the walls; a thick green mildew stinking of decay. Vibrant tapestries also felt the touch of darkness, their once bright colors now dulled in shades of grey and black and patches of infected green that worsened as the long seconds rolled by. She slowed to a stilted jog, looking about herself. Breath plumed in front of her face, lingering and expanding into the bitter ice cold that had nothing to do with the Welsh winter.

What is this thing? Emrysa knew of no dark power

that could consume all life and light. Not that she knew *that* much about the dark arts, but she would have been a fool not to know *something*—not to gather an understanding of what's out there in the world, what she might need to know to defend herself, defend her brother. Her *family*. Not that the knowledge had saved her family. In the end, to save herself, she had brought this thing back. And it had killed her parents. It may as well have been by her very own hand, she thought with ever increasing pain and guilt. Oh yes, she knew what darkness was now—its weight pressed down on her, making her insides ache.

The corridors, the chambers, they were all empty. Besides the darkened touch, there was nothing.

Where is everybody?

Had they run for cover? Did they escape before the Darkness took hold? There were no bodies—she shivered at the memory of her parents' massacred bodies.

The castle was a ghost's shadow.

"I don't like this, I don't like this one bit," Emrysa muttered as she turned into the dining hall.

She stopped short, her hand shooting to her mouth as bile rose to her throat. With the moon a little higher in the sky now, casting its glow through the tall windows, she had just enough light to see what she wished she could not. Holding her breath and pinching her nostrils, Emrysa tiptoed to two maids face down on the flagstones. She knelt, squirming with a gulp as she turned the redhead's cold body over. It wasn't Rhian, and she breathed only a small sigh of relief. She knew she shouldn't have favorites but that didn't stop the feeling that the young maid was the closest thing to a sister Emrysa had ever had. Pale dead eyes stared back at her, and at once Emrysa felt guilt for her thoughts. Nobody deserved to die like this. Especially these girls. *Girls.* Younger than her by years, never to know life or freedom. Both dead. Brutally, savagely murdered.

Emrysa backed away from the horror, from the morbid impossibility of it all. A rare moment where she wished to have her father's men—his warriors—close.

She made her way to the main hall now, hoping in vain to see a sign of life instead of the consuming emptiness. Hoping to find her father's men. Hoping and not hoping to find the Darkness. On the threshold, Emrysa paused, wondering for a moment if she should wait for the others. Even Nimue's help would be appreciated if the Darkness was hiding in the room before her. But her curiosity won out. And on impulse, she shuffled forward.

The showpiece of the main hall, the golden oak, was still standing. Just.

But where hours ago the branches were thick and

full of golden leaves, laden with ripe fruit, now it stood bare. As naked as Emrysa's fears. She could see it in the shadows if she looked closely, the way the empty branches now crumbled, turning to ash. The floor knee-deep with fallen leaves, but these were not the fallen leaves of autumn, crisp and golden. These leaves were as sharp and as black as broken promises. As black as a raven's heart. It was as if the golden oak had been replaced by another tree altogether.

And then she remembered. She had seen trees like this before.

In the world through the portal.

Leaves crunched behind her, she spun.

"It is not completely your fault," Merlin said, looking in horror at the dying tree. "I should have been quicker to grab you, or I should have ensured a spell to only allow beings from this world back in. You cannot blame yourself entirely."

Emrysa scoffed, because she did not blame herself entirely. In fact, now she thought about it, she did not blame herself one bit. If the stupid Council had just left her and her brother to their own devices and not planned her murder, none of this would have happened.

Her parents would still be alive. Her maids. Her dragon heart... her soul would still be whole.

"Whatever this is, Merlin, it is not my fault," Emrysa

began, dead leaves disintegrating beneath her feet as she placed her palm upon the dying golden oak. A sickly feeling came over her—the silent screams nestled within the death trees of the other world. "But I do intend to fix it."

"How?!" Merlin barked. "If our powers combined could not stop it, what makes you so sure you can alone?"

Emrysa turned away with a shrug. She didn't know, except she had a feeling in her bones, deep in the marrow of her being that she must do something. A heaviness brewed, one that said everything, *everyone*, whether they knew it or not, whether they *believed* her or not, were reliant upon her next move.

"I'll make a plan, find a spell. I always do." She started toward Merlin, but her eyes tore from his to the view over his shoulder. "What's going on?"

They both turned to the window.

Torches, dozens of them, on the far horizon. By the way the lights bounced, they belonged to horsemen. They were coming a clip, whoever they were.

"Our townsfolk seeking safety here, no doubt," Emrysa said, but Nimue burst through the shadows, Dermot in tow.

"Emrysa!" Nimue said. "It's the Council."

"Here to help? Finally, they do something positive for

this family," Emrysa said, surprisingly hopeful. But Nimue's face was twisted in a painful grimace.

Dermot cast his eyes to his feet, his complexion paler than ever. "Nimue and I, we've... we've seen something —in the scrying board."

Merlin shot Nimue a stern stare. Emrysa looked between the two. It was Nimue who pushed past Merlin to grab Emrysa's hands.

"I've just been in communication with the Council— while you made your way here—I *had* to. We need their help."

Emrysa frowned. "We do, but it doesn't make sense. How can they be here so quickly?"

"They were already close... to prepare for your..."

"Execution?"

Nimue looked away and Emrysa wondered if it was through shame or guilt, or both.

"The Council know of the Darkness, Emrysa," Nimue continued. "They are coming to eradicate it." Her fingers, as cold as steel, clenched around Emrysa's own.

"Okay, so grievances forgotten for now, I'll help them—help you." She turned to Merlin. "If it means we can get rid of this *thing.*"

"Emrysa," Nimue shook her head. "They are not only planning to eradicate the Darkness. They plan to eradicate you as well."

"What on hell fire?!" Merlin yelled, breaking between the two. "What have you told them? What have you done?!"

"I didn't need to tell them anything for them to know! The Darkness has already spread across the kingdom. I'm only telling you what they told me through the scrying board."

"Well, what did they say?" demanded Emrysa.

"They're blaming you for unleashing the Darkness. They think you killed your parents too—"

"But that's ridiculous! We'll tell them, *show them*, when they get here. And then I can, I don't know, make them believe me."

Nimue shook her head. "They will not wait to ask questions, Emrysa. They have commanded me to ensure we have you ready."

"Ready for what?" Dermot asked.

"To… to be condemned."

Dermot hissed through his teeth. Merlin kicked up the dead leaves in frustration.

Emrysa raged. "Why are you telling me this? You of all people?"

"You know why," Nimue said, her stare ardent. She licked her lips reminding Emrysa of the stolen kiss. "I was sent here to do a job. I didn't expect to feel anything about the mission. I didn't expect to feel anything toward *you...*"

Emrysa stood stunned.

"Here, let me show you," Nimue said finally.

Nimue cleared the leaves, exposing dying sap that seeped across the floor like thick tar. It was enough liquid to replay the scrying scene she and Dermot had seen only moments before. Though the images were far from clear, the voices rang as true as death.

15

THE PROTECTORS OF MAGIC

"*T*his is our opportunity, we all know this, do we not?" A wizened woman said, her voice as cold as steel.

She addressed a long, narrow table full of witches and wizards and other beings—half-animal, half-human. Things Emrysa had never before seen. She stepped forward, bending closer to the vision before her.

"What are they?' Dermot asked, but Emrysa hushed him with a single finger to her lips. She couldn't miss a word.

"The Cheval bloodline has caused nothing but controversy for centuries—"

"By being powerful wielders of magic?" One young witch pitched in. "Is that what this is about? Power?"

"Oh goodness. She's pretty," Dermot mused aloud, earning a dig in the ribs from Emrysa's elbow.

"We cannot have one family wield more power than the entire Alchive Council!" the first witch roared, pounding the table with her fist to better make her point. All jumped, but the young witch.

"I was sworn into the Council to protect the very people you are trying to condemn. Are we not meant to be the protectors of magic? Therefore, the protectors of the very beings who wield it?"

"She's wonderful," Dermot said dreamily. Emrysa flapped her hand to quieten him as the old witch pointed a finger to the girl, and with one slice through the air, silenced the witch. Her lips melded together until they were no longer there.

Neat spell, Emrysa thought with an arching eyebrow, and tucked the knowledge away in her arsenal.

"Something has happened, something... dark," the old witch began. "Something that has altered the course of the future, and our future within it. What has happened has marked a turning point. From now on, everything in our world is insecure."

Nobody spoke; the delay so long that Emrysa wondered if the scrying board had stuck in one place. However, just before she dipped her finger in the blooded tree sap to restart the vision, somebody else spoke up. A middle-aged man who still possessed a teenage look of innocence in his dark eyes.

"What would you mean by *'our future?'*"

"The future of witches, the future of magic."

The room in the scrying board hushed. As did the witches staring into the vision.

"If we do it now, now while we have the opportunity, we can turn this prophecy around. We can claim our place in the future, ensure witches will not become extinct. Ensure *magic* will not become extinct." The old witch looked at each Alchive Council member in turn, allowing the gravitas of her words to sink in. She undid her silencing spell but the young pretty witch remained quiet all the same, taking in the words, taking in the impossibility of a world without magic.

A world without magic? Emrysa's heart clenched.

"Then pray tell us, what would you have us do?" The pretty witch asked, but everybody already knew the answer.

The old witch spoke again, and when she did, it was if the very chords of nature clung to her words. "To stop this terrible future from transpiring, we need to kill the cause at the root. We need to kill the Golden Oak. We need kill the Cheval bloodline dead. And we need to kill them *tonight*. For *this* is the prophecy I have seen."

The old witch hammered her hands together and a

clap of thunder reverberated across the room, across time and space through the scrying board. Her ancient hands palled apart an image, shaking and blurry that grew on the canvas of the air above the long dining table. And then it cleared. The prophecy there, for all to see...

16

THE PROPHECY

*R*ose stood at the water's edge, hands splayed by her sides, face upturned toward the moon. An untrained eye would see an old woman dreaming of golden days once passed. But the old woman was not looking into the past—she was staring into the future.

Her faraway gaze remained fixed, unblinking. Eyes glazed with a pale white film—a shimmering glow as if the moon itself shone from them. The art of scrying was all but lost to modern witches, but Rose was no modern witch. Her blood boiled with her ancestor's powers and time did little to weaken them. Despite her frail form—back hunched, knuckles gnarled, and fingers twisted—the moon listened intently to Rose's commands. Its pallid light reflected upon the witch and the midnight-blue lake. It shared its secrets, shared its knowledge—it shared the future.

Rose gasped; her eyes flinging open as she reached for a heavy pendant nestled over her heart. She looked around herself, startled as if waking from a nightmare. Her fingers trembled with magic... with knowledge.

"The prophecy," she whispered, nodding thanks to the moon as it slunk behind a blackened cloud.

She lifted the hem of her skirt, flitting from the riverside as fast as her frail legs could muster. Her ragged breath caught in her throat, but panting, she continued through the woods. In the darkness, branches struck her face but her urgency was too great to stop and she cast a parting spell. Clouds, their outlines illuminated by the moon's secret, rumbled and darkened. Electricity—the conduit upon which magic travels—prickled in the old woman's blood.

She didn't have much time.

Lightning crackled, illuminating the sky with a simultaneous roar of thunder.

The magic of the world would soon be lost and with it, everything the world held dear. It was a price Rose was willing to pay but she knew she would have to pay with more. For the moon's secret, Rose would pay with her life. It would be the first of many lives lost to the prophecy. The war on witches was about to commence.

Nobody was safe.

Magic, for all its beauty, power and grace, would have to die.

17

A NEW DIRECTION

"*T*hat has to be the biggest load of horseshit I've ever heard!" Emrysa stamped her foot into the vision, and the images rippled away to reveal nothing but the flagstones. "Nonsense. Absolute nonsense. As if magic could be taken from the world, as if I'd have a hand to play in it. Who is this *Rose* woman anyway? What the hell has she got to do with me?"

Emrysa continued rambling. The images made no sense, the words, the tales, the prophecy. *What even is electricity?* Magic was shaped by will and nature, wasn't it? *Wasn't it?*

"We have to get you somewhere safe," Merlin began.

"Aren't you listening to me?" Emrysa yelled. "It's utter rubbish."

"It doesn't matter what is true, Emrysa," Merlin said. "What matters is what people *believe.*"

The terrible truth of his words hung heavy in the air.

"What he says is right," Nimue butted in. "People—*witches*—will be scared, they'll believe whatever lies promise to keep them safe. Witches might not love the Alchive Council, I know that only too well, but they do trust their ability to protect them from harm."

"Shit," Emrysa said again, then, turning to her brother. "I'm so sorry this has happened, it *is* all my fault—"

"I am the dunderhead who opened the portal with little more than alchemy and senselessness. I should never have done it; this wouldn't have happened if I just allowed you the time to work out your own spell."

Emrysa took his hand, and even with her heavy heart and fraying soul, she could not bring herself to tell him what she believed. Yes, perhaps it was his fault. If he had only given her the time to work out another spell. Regardless of her thoughts, she squeezed his fingers gently and offered him a wan smile.

"Come Dermot, we'll saddle the horses, we'll ride away. And then we'll find a way to fix this, fix the Darkness, the mess."

"I'm coming with you," Merlin said.

But Emrysa shook her head. "No, Merlin. It's too

dangerous. I need someone who knows what has happened here—to share my truth so one day someone will believe me. And if the Council get me... I need someone to tell my side of the story. People need to know what happened to the Chevals." She stared deep into his eyes. "Merlin, will you tell my story?"

He paused. "I *am* your story, Emrysa. Take me with you. We can work this out *together*."

Emrysa wished to either slap his stupid face or kiss those beautiful lips, she couldn't decide, so drawn to him she was, it made her angry. It simply wasn't fair to find someone like this, now, when her entire future was unravelling.

Nimue stepped between them, cool and calm as always. "Enough." Her icy stare penetrated Emrysa like her tongue had earlier in the evening, but her eyes were rimmed with something... something *else*. What was it? Jealousy? Defeat? Heartbreak?

"Merlin, you will stay here with me, we can stall the Council, give the Chevals time." She turned to Emrysa now, her stare longing. Pleading. "Go, I know of a place where it will be hard for them to find you. A place that will conceal you. At least give you time—or us time—to figure out our next move."

"But what about the Darkness?" Emrysa asked.

"The Council will find a way to work it all out, they

always do," Nimue said. "But I won't let them take you. Now, go! Saddle the horses, command the faerie roads. There's a cave to the west of the Winterlands. Ride like lightning and keep in mind a place to scry so we can contact you when we have any information."

Emrysa nodded, heart thudding.

"But—" Merlin said.

"There's no time for discussion," Nimue pressed. "They are *coming*."

The thud of horses' hooves grew ever closer. The pounding of the castle door in the distance. The demand to open at once.

The Council were not coming.

They were here.

It was Nimue who grabbed Emrysa and kissed her ardently as Merlin watched on dumbfounded.

"Go!" Nimue said. "Save yourself."

SWORN WITH OATH

*E*mrysa pulled herself away from Nimue and stole one last glance at Merlin's face, before spinning to see only Dermot's terrified eyes.

"Quickly, through the tunnels," she hissed.

And in a second the siblings were gone, disappearing though a hidden trapdoor and fleeing through the underground tunnels made to protect the family if under attack from warfare. It was here she found them —the women who kept the castle household running, the men sworn with oath and heart to protect their lord and kin.

"It's a massacre." The words slipped unbidden from Emrysa as she stood upon piles of bloodied, dead bodies. A river of blood ran through the cylindrical passageway as she and Dermot tripped and sloshed their way through the mold-covered tunnels. The touch of Darkness ever-present despite their flame spells lighting the way.

"They must have tried to flee, only to get caught. But what does it gain from killing?" Emrysa asked, helpless.

Dermot ignored her question. "I cannot believe this to be our fate." Dermot tripped over a body whose face was covered in shadow and blood. He didn't dare look back, he didn't dare look down... he would not allow himself to recognize the faces of the men and women he had known his entire life now dead beneath his feet. He wouldn't allow himself to imagine that amongst them could be the sweet, Rhian. *Where had she gone?*

"I won't let this be our fate, Dermot," Emrysa said, pinning her eyes ahead, neither daring to glance down at the soft bodies she tread upon in their escape. "I've told you before, I'll do anything to protect you, and brother—" She stopped now, spinning to face him. "If I have to sacrifice myself to do that, I will. Know that."

"No!" Dermot whispered as urgently as a whisper would allow. They could both hear footsteps above them, could both feel the force of the magic held in that space. The Council was close. "*You* are the one with the most power, it should be me sacrificing myself for you.

You need to keep our bloodlines going, I have nothing to offer the future other than alchemy and silence. You have so much more."

"That's ridiculous."

"No, Emrysa. It's the truth. You know the truth is hard to hear, even harder to accept. But know I will, if the time comes. You have to keep our story going."

They shared but a moment of gratitude; gratitude for the unflinching love they felt for one another... yet there was a lingering worry in the pit of Emrysa's stomach.

What if the Darkness did pull me under its spell? What if, without my dragon heart, without my soul intact, the Darkness wins me over? No, Emrysa knew exactly who had to be the one to survive if all this went wrong. She smiled at her doe-eyed brother with his soft heart and kind mind, and was momentarily pleased that at least it was she who had to sacrifice so much of herself. She couldn't imagine a world in which her brother was forced to experience the dull ache as she did. She wished to send him a soothing spell, as she had done only hours before when the entire world was different, but with the Council so close, she daren't. Instead, she threw a half-smile before they ran again, over bodies of the men who had succumbed to the Darkness that had encroached their castle, their lives.

But where is the thing now? Emrysa wondered. And what would be waiting for them as they escaped the clutches of the Council and fled into the throes of the darkness beyond?

19

MIDNIGHT STEALTH

*E*mrysa knew the underground tunnels like the freckles upon her nose. She had spent her childhood playing games of hide and seek, or chase, or simply running from her parents when she was in trouble, to find some peace in the stables. The farther they went, the less bodies they found, until there was nothing but a constant black hole ahead and echoing drips, hollow and tinny in the dank subterranean air. Still, left turns, right turns, straight aheads, Emrysa knew them all until she found the wall ladder that would lead them to the trapdoor to the stable.

"Maybe I should go first," Dermot suggested.

Emrysa screwed her face up at him. "Why would you do that? I'm the eldest, and the eldest always goes first, remember?"

"Factually, we've discovered that's not actually true."

Of course, Emrysa conceded the truth, but not the argument. "I always go first, there's no need to become the big brave brother now you've discovered you *are* my big brother."

Dermot almost smiled. "It's not that, you almighty plum. It's just you're still wearing your nightdress and quite frankly, I don't want to see what's under there if I climb the ladder behind you. I've seen enough masses of darkness to last me a lifetime."

Despite everything, Emrysa barked a laugh. "Here, will this do?" She swiveled her hand around her body and incanted beneath her breath, content that they were far enough from the castle for the Council not to feel her magic. But her magic was different from before, when she had a full soul. Not stronger but...

Her nightdress morphed from the blood and gore splattered white to shades of black, shiny as a raven's eye. The material clung to her like a second skin, to every contour of her skin.

"By the Goddess, Emrysa?!" Dermot looked wide eyed.

It was not what Emrysa had planned. She had wanted an outfit to help her agility to escape with stealth in the darkness. She looked down at herself in shock. Emrysa had never before worn men's trousers, only they were *not* men's. They clung to her—a thick, supple, and shiny leather as soft as calf skin against her own. No skirts to cover her modesty. And the bodice, instead of hiding flesh, enriched it, highlighting her cinched waist, her full breasts.

"Well," she said, a little lost for words.

Dermot *humphed* with a disapproving older-brother glare that came quite naturally to him, he was pleased to admit.

"Just get up that bloody ladder." He *swooshed* his hand at her, turning away as she raised herself up the first rungs of the ladder, her leather boots thumping upon the wooden steps.

Her fingers trailed a worn symbol engraved into the wood at the ceiling of the tunnel. It glowed a pale blue as she whispered the words she knew so well. It groaned open. Strands of golden straw fell from the barn above their heads, a beautiful color in a world devoid of it.

They raised themselves up, the horses snorting in disgust at being interrupted in their peaceful slumber.

"At least the Darkness hasn't reached here," Emrysa said, helping her brother. "I hadn't even taken that into consideration."

"Don't be so quick to count our blessings, we're yet to know what awaits us outside," Dermot said with grim reality.

"True," Emrysa mused, eyeing the Council's horses—Merlin and Nimue's horses—she wasn't sure if they would be Council members for much longer after tonight. "Come here, boy," she said, clicking her tongue and holding out a hand to the small herd. She magicked up a ripe apple in her palm, and one horse forced its way through the wary beasts, succumbing to her bribe.

Its breath was warm on her skin as it chomped fearlessly, unaware of the task ahead. Its eye, darker than coal, looked up at her through long black eyelashes. The horse was beautiful. A long wavy mane flowed from a thick, muscular crest, trailing past long its shoulder toward its knees. The beast's strong muscles rippled even at rest, and its coat sparkled blacker than a midnight sky, in contrast to the Cheval's white beasts. With any luck, Emrysa thought, they would be hidden away in the night with these horses.

"Come on, sister, there is no time for caressing," Dermot urged, dropping saddlery to the ground with a *whomp.* The horse sensed her sudden anxiety—getting agitated as she rushed to get the bit in the horse's mouth and the headpiece over his ears.

Emrysa tried calming the fidgeting horse as she saddled it, losing her patience when it whinnied and pulled back.

"Stand still, will you?" she scolded, putting a spell in

place to make the horse compliant. It was not a spell she relished but needs must, she considered, and time was precious.

"You know, if you trusted him a little more, he would stay calm for you." Merlin appeared from nowhere, making Emrysa jump and curse.

"By the Goddess? How do you do that?" Emrysa clasped her heart-space. "Anyway, how can I trust a horse I don't know? And how can I trust the beast isn't riddled in magic that will take me to the Council instead of fleeing from them?"

"Oh come on, Emrysa." Merlin shook his head and had the audacity to smile his charming smile. Despite how it made her feel inside, Emrysa refused to smile back.

Merlin's hand soothed the horse's neck, then stroked his forehead under the mass of wavy black forelock. "His name is Protector, and that's exactly what he'll do."

Emrysa shot Merlin a contemptuous galore. "You have to be joking me?"

Merlin laughed, a sound sending calmness and elation through Emrysa's veins at the same time. "His name is Bruce, but it hardly seems like a gallant name for a steed galloping under the stealth of midnight."

Merlin smiled again, the charming rascal, then laughed. It was a beautiful sound and Emrysa wished she could have heard it before, when her world and life wasn't in danger, when her heart still pounded strong and her aura still pulsed with the fiery red that matched his own. Now her aura pulsed with deep burgundy that started to darken to black at the edges.

"Nice outfit," Merlin chimed in, with a comical expression. Dermot groaned in the background and mumbled something inaudible under his breath.

Emrysa did smile then. "I suppose you're right—about the horse's name, I mean. Not the outfit. But I like it... the horse, I mean. *Shit*." Emrysa stopped to catch her breath, wondering why she babbled so much just because Merlin was close to her. "Bruce," she said, trying to catch her breath. "It's a name that sounds true."

"As am I—to you." Merlin grabbed Emrysa's hand and pressed it against his heart. She could feel it pound double-time under her palm, pulsing with life and wonder. She looked away, unwilling to lose herself in those intense hazel eyes.

"In another life," she said, closing her eyes not to see his reaction.

"No," Merlin said, steadfast. "This life. This life is ours and I promise, no matter what, I'm with you. No matter what happens. No matter the darkness of the future. I'm yours."

"You say this as a *promise*?"

"Sealed with a kiss."

Merlin leant down to Emrysa. She felt his skin on her own, smelt his warm musky sent. First, he kissed her forehead, then traced the contours of her temple, her cheeks. When he found her lips, Emrysa found herself hungry for his kiss. Hungry for him, his world. And the entire world shrank to the space between them.

She could live like this. She knew it in her marrow. She would love this man forever, past lives and generations and universes coming and going. It was a love lit up.

A love that could never die—no matter what.

Tears touched her eyelashes and her empty heart nearly exploded with the emotion it tried to contain. It was as if Merlin's love made her heart whole again. Perhaps his soul could do the same, she hoped, with every fiber of her being.

"You can count on me," Merlin promised again. Ardent. And Emrysa, with all her heart, believed him.

"I hate to be a glorified pooper of all parties, but dear love-sick, slightly cringe-worthy lovebirds, we *have* to get moving," Dermot said, flushing red with an embarrassment neither Merlin nor Emrysa witnessed as they continued to stare deeply into each other's souls. "*Come on*, chippy-chop and all. Darkness waits for no man, or woman, or whatever. *Emrysa*, tear yourself away, dear child. It's not a good look on you. I far better prefer the sullen, supercilious air of contempt you usually wear, and your usual clothes too, come to that matter."

Emrysa huffed, then smirked, then kissed Merlin one more time and with that kiss she pressed all her emotions into him so he could never lose them. So he could feel them, forever, no matter her fate.

She would not be forgotten.

The horses whinnied, tense, and a dread filled Emrysa's fraying soul. A recognition. A knowing.

It seeped through, the Darkness, crawling along the walls with its cold, damp, mildew, turning the golden straw in the barn to blackened ash. Eyes white with fear, Bruce began pulling away.

"There is no time, you have to go!" Merlin ordered, legging Emrysa onto his horse. He slapped its rump. "Go!"

Emrysa pulled back on the reins as the horse lunged forward, forcing Bruce to fidget beneath her. "But what about you, in this darkness, what will you—"

"Go!" Merlin ordered and with that, he swiveled his hand around his head and shoulders and was gone.

Dermot stared, gobsmacked. Even he knew that a magic that could transport was nearly unnatural, even for the whimsical laws of magic. The siblings shared a quick glance. There was time for nothing else.

"Ya!" Emrysa roared a split second later, digging her heels into Bruce's flanks. But she needn't have bothered. Both Council horses could not wait to escape the Darkness.

"*Apart!*" she yelled, and the barn doors crashed open to her spell. And with the sound of pounding hooves and hearts, the Chevals galloped from the barn into the night.

20

CLARITY

They galloped through the open pastures hard beneath hoof with frost, and under the stealth of night, headed toward the forests that fringed the coastline.

"The beach," Emrysa called over her shoulder, breathless. "We'll make more time across the beach."

"But we'll be exposed! We should remain in the woods under cover," Dermot said.

She conceded, and they entered the forest. Aromas of pine and dirt wafted upwards as hooves cut through the ice atop thick, sloppy mud. They slowed, the *slurp* of thick mud sucking and pulling at the horses' hooves and fetlocks.

"We need to get off the main path if we want dryer ground," Emrysa said over her shoulder, cursing the scars of a wet and frosty Welsh winter. They scrambled to uneven ground between the trees, thick and dense now as they rode from the main path. They picked up speed causing branches to whip at their ice-stung faces. The dark and uneven terrain topped with frost made the horses slip and stumble and lose ground time and again. They pressed on, hunched low over the beasts' shoulders, protecting their faces from branch welts and putting all their trust in the animals beneath them.

Look after us, Emrysa thought into the mind of Bruce.

As you will us, Bruce thought into her mind. There was no need for anymore conversation, they *knew* each other's thoughts. *Felt* each other's thoughts. They pressed on in the gloom and the icy fog that formed and snaked its way through the trees.

A sudden shriek, and Emrysa gasped, dreading the arrival of the dark.

"Emrysa!" called Dermot.

It wasn't the Darkness; it was Dermot's horse falling. Her brother crashed to the ground beside the beast, and it rolled, scrambled to stand, and shook its body—indignant.

"Shit!" Emrysa cursed, spinning Bruce around. "Are you okay? Is the horse okay?"

Dermot was quick to rise from the forest loam and

the horse, although blowing and agitated, was free of any cuts or lameness.

"We're okay," Dermot conceded. "But you're right, *again.* We should head to the beach."

The sandy track was hard going, a steep craggy decline filled deep with soft sand and jutted turrets and loose boulders made it slow work—the horses needing to sit right back on their haunches to gain balance and purchase as they slid downward, Emrysa and Dermot leaning right back to help better balance the steeds beneath them. But on they went until the crescendo of crashing waves could be heard beyond the sandbanks— the roaring coastline of a king tide.

The predawn coastline awaited—majestic and mysterious.

A path opened to the expanse of sand stretching as far as the eye could see, while sea-fret whipped from the surging waves pounding the shore; the sand both soft and firm beneath the horses' hooves. Wind stole their breath.

The high full moon offered little light as the shadows upon horseback rode onto the black night-time sand. The saddlery creaked and groaned with the horses' prancing anticipation—the only sound bar a horse snort over the battle of wind and shore.

Emrysa took a deep breath, checking over her

shoulder to ensure nobody had followed, then looked ahead, choosing their escape. A violent red slash stained the horizon as dawn promised its approach—a deep, expansive blood stain across the swirling ocean. Emrysa bit her lip, hoping this image was not a sign dictating her future.

Like an urgent whisper, they galloped along the shoreline, frigid water spraying from hooves, manes and tails flailing with the wild winds. The lazy sun began to rise as they sped across the sand, casting golden-red rays of light before them. Emrysa turned to look behind her. The wind ceased as she did so, to allow the sound of pounding hooves and the blowing breath of her horse. She couldn't work out if the darkness behind them was land yet untouched by dawn, or the land in the grips of the otherworldly emptiness spreading from her castle. Then she saw it.

The mass of darkness swirling up to the sky above their home.

"No!" Emrysa screamed, pulling the reins hard. Bruce reared to a stop, throwing his head in retaliation against the sharp metal pull in his mouth. She spun him around, Dermot already slowing to join her.

"Is that..." Dermot trailed off.

Emrysa watched, wide-eyed. The way the black darted and danced with the rhythm of the wind. It *wasn't* the Darkness. It was smoke. An incredible amount of smoke billowing into the sky. And the truth hit Emrysa in the pit of her fraying soul.

"Our home! They're burning our home to the ground!" Emrysa watched as everything she knew was licked with fire and flame. Smoke spiraled from windows, flames from others. And just as the smoke curled into the air, so too, the Darkness along the black and dying sand. It tugged at her soul, beckoned her, seduced her. Emrysa pushed her horse toward both, despite Bruce's protests.

"Emrysa, what are you *doing*?" Dermot yelled. "There's nothing we can do. Nothing to go back for. We have to save ourselves. Come on!"

But his voice was like a fractured memory or dream, too far away to allow the words to ring true. Something else felt true though, the Darkness. Again, she pushed her horse forward then gasped.

"Dermot, my grimoire. I have to go back. I have to save it!"

Dermot's bottom jaw nearly fell from his face with the force of his surprise. "*Your grimoire?* Are you serious?! Of all things to go back for, you think you need your spellbook? You don't even need it to make spells work!"

Emrysa fought with the truth of his words and the

feeling in her marrow. "I can't explain it, but I have to. I just have a feeling, a really bad feeling that if I don't get that book, something... something *awful* will happen. Something irreversible."

"Well I can tell you something awful will happen if you do go back for it, you dunderheaded nitwit! *Come on.* Leave it, let's go."

But Emrysa refused. It suddenly felt like the most important thing in the world to do, to have that book.

"Go, follow the faerie roads to the Winterlands." But Dermot shook his head. "I'll catch you up. I promise just... *please!*"

"No. No way," Dermot said sternly. "If you're going back then so, too, am I. I'm not just going to leave you!"

"Dermot, they're more likely to discover two than one. And besides, my magic is *strong.*" She didn't want to hurt his feelings, but it was the only way he might listen. "What hope would you have if you needed to use your magic to protect yourself against the Council? And you'll slow me down," Emrysa hated herself for saying it. "I'll have to protect both of us because your magic won't be able to protect you."

Dermot's face dropped. Emrysa had been the only one who had ever abstained from bringing to light his magical disadvantages. He was wordless and it broke Emrysa's heart. She bit her trembling lip. "Please, please look after yourself. I'll meet you there. I'll see you in the Winterlands, I promise."

Watching her brother turn and tear away toward the blood-stained horizon alone was one of the hardest things she ever had to do, but there was certain magic that could not be ignored. The magic of foresight, and it pulsed around her now in the nonsensical way foresight does. She knew not *why* she had to do it, only that she did, and she galloped back along the shoreline to the burning ruins of her home. Hoping it was not too late to save the spellbook. Hoping the Council had already gone. Hoping Merlin had not gone back on his promise.

Hoping the Darkness would not take her as its claws sank into her skin and flesh.

21

FIRE AND FLAME

Stealth was not needed when Emrysa found her way back to the burning castle, that much was clear. The Council were nowhere to be seen, and the only company she had besides her horse, was the choking ashes and remains of her parents sticking to her lungs. The castle had become a funeral pyre—for her parents, for all the kind and brave souls who had lived and worked there... died there, because of what *she* had brought back into their world. The flames roared, louder than the ocean ever had. And Emrysa watched, hands clasped to her chest, tears tracking down her soot-covered face.

She said a prayer.

Promised a vendetta.

The Council would pay.

The Darkness thundered around her and she grasped it, holding it tight against her soul, feeling its protection from the pain that threatened to render her senseless. The grimoire. That was all she needed here. Leave the memories and the love and the emotion for another time.

Covering her mouth with her hands she coughed and spluttered as she rounded the back of the ruined building, hoping to find a stairway or a turret unaffected by the flames.

The first turret had already tumbled to the ground, the flames having devoured the internal wooden structure to leave the mortar to crumble and the stones to fall. The second turret had flames licking from every window—from the bottom floor to the highest room that acted as a lookout. The eaves, the floors, the tapestries upon the wall, all acting as kindle for the flames.

But flames had yet to reach the third turret, so she raced toward it, hoping to outrun the fire's wrath. Around and around she climbed, higher and higher, her hand supporting herself on the wooden handrail she knew would be the stairs' downfall in time. Coughing and spluttering all the while, she burst into her study, taking one last look at anything familiar left before it, too, would burst into flames before her.

She found the book exactly where she'd left it. Her fingers traced the leather tome with something that resembled reverence, and she spoke the words as she felt them tingle beneath her fingertips.

"The Cheval Book of Shadows."

She opened it, laughing gently at some of her earlier spells, her smile fading as she flicked through the pages revealing more mature, complex spells, and spells warding against darkness. She never thought she would need one to ward off the Alchive Council themselves. If only she knew then, if only she had the time to summon a protection spell against them.

"Wait, wait!" She felt her foresight come and go like dreams in the morning light. She needed to grapple it, pin it down, find the words as she would a poem just out of reach. There were spells that needed completing. Spells that needed adjusting. New spells. Summoning spells.

Emrysa had no clue as to why she would need to do this, only a certainty in her soul that she must. She scrambled through the smoke to find her ink and quill, the ink bubbling with heat, and desperately, she wrote in the margins of the book, adapting the spells to become stronger.

She wrote like a demon, words rendered almost unreadable with her haste. But quicker, she continued.

"Damn!" In her rush, Emrysa knocked over the pot of ink, a black puddle leaking and sizzling across the hot floor covered in mold and darkness.

"No, no, no, no!" she screamed. This spell she had to write, to finish, to adapt. She opened a random page with wide margins, stabbed the quill into the soft underside of her arm and dragged it downwards to her wrist.

Emrysa bit back her yelp, but still sobbed as red swelled from her incision. Her body shuddered with pain, with disgust, torment, urgency. She had to do this. And with her blood, she wrote the spell she somehow knew she would need to rely upon in the future, somewhere, somehow. A word formed in her mind, not her voice nor the voice of her thoughts, something else.

Fire Heart, it whispered. She looked around at the blaze and smoke. *You need a Fire Heart.* Emrysa wondered if this name was to be hers, given to her by magic and nature itself, or someone else. Someone who could help her. The *only* person who could help her.

A loud crash brought her out of her thoughts. The falling of the Golden Oak in the main hall. She felt it combust and for a reason she couldn't fathom, this saddened her more than anything else. Their reign was over. Their power cut short if the rumors were true. Ash wafted like snow; smoke curled its way toward her. Darkness tempted her soul. But Emrysa resisted.

Hugging the book close and spilling her blood along the pages. Task complete, she galloped down the spiral stairway, wondering if she was spiraling to her own descent.

She found Bruce where she left him, of course, she had compelled him. She'd had to. She hated herself for it, but he was too nervous to stay. Emrysa mounted him in one swift movement, and they galloped on toward her brother and the twisting, cruel uncertainty of the faerie roads.

22

THE FAERIE ROADS

*E*mrysa neither liked nor trusted the faerie roads. She had studied them enough, she had no choice, it was compulsory education at the Cheval household. There was a reason—many reasons—why nobody had entered them for centuries. It was an unnatural place that lead to capricious places, so all the more reason to study. All the more reason to go. The Council would not consider the faerie roads as a well-executed escape plan. Begrudgingly, Emrysa knew she had Nimue —the strange creature—to thank for that.

She slowed Bruce to a walk through a craggy pass, where cavernous stones loomed over them full of spiteful threats. Emrysa pulled the grimoire closer to her body for safety. Like the Forest Black, leafless trees bowed down to meet her here and there. Her mind's eye played tricks on her, seeing once more those terrifying silent screams etched into the bark, but no such thing existed here. Still, breath tight, Emrysa shook her head, feeling an unnatural coldness on the roads as nature bent around her. Bruce was sure and steadfast, thank the Goddess, his hooves dodging the deep crevasses and finding purchase as he slipped and scrambled over slick moss-covered stones in ice cold riverbeds.

Where is he? Emrysa cast a finding spell to help locate her brother. He was close, she gleaned that much, but with the faerie roads' strange and sinister magic wrapped tightly around her own, finding his exact location proved impossible. But she kept riding toward the *feeling* of him.

She rounded the corner.

"I hate the Winterlands," Emrysa hissed, taking in the immense plateau that spanned the endless horizon. Empty and desolate, the place gave her a feeling of hopelessness deeper than she had ever before felt. They wouldn't stay here long, Emrysa promised herself. Despite Nimue's best intentions to keep them safe, the Winterlands came with its own version of condemnation, one Emrysa wanted no part of.

"Dermot?" she called in vain, her voice fragile within the expanse of nothingness. Two ravens cawed, perched upon a naked branch above.

She gulped, and kicked Bruce along. On they walked, heading west toward the mountain peaks towering over the wasteland. Its shadow engulfed them, and its size rendered them insignificant. And although she knew the Alchive Council would not be aware of her presence here, and although the urgency of fleeing had, for the moment at least, ebbed, Emrysa couldn't help but feel on edge. Watched. *Seen.*

Eventually Dermot's presence led her to a small opening, a dark hole hidden within the base of the mountain.

This must be the cave of which Nimue spoke. Every part of her body and soul, heart and mind, warned her not to enter. All but one, the one that sensed her brother's presence within. She dismounted, her feet and ankles tingling as she landed with the cold, so she had to hobble a few steps before the feeling came back to her. She tied Bruce to a skeletal tree near the entrance before hovering at the threshold.

"Damn it," she cursed after a long while, and entered.

Immediately, darkness engulfed her, leaving her blind. She tiptoed a few paces, hands feeling the way ahead, the walls slick with wet and damp. The air heavy, dense, making it difficult to breathe.

"Dermot?" She spoke into the cavernous hole. Nothing but the *plonk* of water dripping. Timidly, she lit a flame to her fingers, pulling a face at the grime it allowed her to see. She could feel Dermot, a whisper of him—a strange sensation. His life force was usually so strong, so connected to one another this spell never failed her. Now, she grappled at the edges trying to pull the faint feeling of him close. She wondered if this was the result of her soul spell. The disconnect not only to herself but her twin. She blew out hard at the thought.

There was shuffling ahead of her in the darkness. Emrysa stopped short. "Who's there?" she demanded, pulling her fear deep inside. "Dermot?"

The shuffling did not stop, and Emrysa, though standing still, leant toward the sound, peering hard into the black ahead.

"Hello?" she called again, her voice muted by the damp enclosure surrounding her.

Again, the shuffling, the sound changing. Footsteps.

A bright purple light erupted. Emrysa jumped, then exhaled slowly.

"Nimue!" she said, relief pooling over Emrysa. "You got here! Where's Dermot? Merlin?"

Nimue's greedy eyes lingered over Emrysa's body in her leather attire. She licked her lips before her features pinched slightly, yet she offered no answers to Emrysa's questions but had an urgency of her own.

"Quickly, come. It's your brother."

"What?" Emrysa shrieked, wide-eyed. "What's wrong with him."

"I'll answer en-route, come on. He needs your help."

They raced along the corridors, both using their flames to light the way. Upon the wall, their tall shadows chased them as they ran deeper into the belly of the hovel.

"Is it the Council? Have they got to him? Do they know we're here?" Emrysa's questions tumbled from her mouth as fast as her feet covered the rank ground. She didn't worry about avoiding the putrid puddles. She barely noticed they were there.

"It's not the Council," Nimue said, turning her head to Emrysa as they ran side-by-side. "It's something else."

"What then? Goddess damn it! Where's Merlin? Is he with Dermot? Is he helping?"

"Don't worry about Merlin. It's your brother who needs your thoughts."

Down they ran, deeper and deeper, the air heavier and heavier until the came into the great expanse—the dark heart of the cave.

"What the..." Emrysa trailed off. First her eyes were drawn to the monolithic fountain at the center, flowing with a dark and metallic twang of...

"Is that... *blood?*" Emrysa said, noticing the huge base of the fountain made entirely by skulls. Then her eyes trailed away to the ground, following the path of a smaller, thinner, fresher trail of blood.

She felt her world stop spinning, felt her fraying soul darkening.

"Dermot!"

23

REVELATIONS

*O*f all the death and darkness Emrysa had ever seen. Of all the fear she felt when lost to the Forest Black and its terrifying essence. Of all the dread of the Darkness as it leaked into her world, killing her parents and everything she had ever known. Nothing —*nothing*—could prepare her for the sight that now stained her eyes and broke her heart.

"No!" She roared, fear paralyzing her.

The details formed in but a second. The five-pointed star, smeared with blood along the ground, the candles flickering black flames at each point. The bulk of her brother's body at the center curled into a fetal position.

So this is why I can only feel a whisper of his presence.

"He's dying?" Emrysa said. A question. A *statement.* She turned to Nimue. "Who... how? Who did this?"

Nimue did not answer and Emrysa didn't wait for her as clarity overcame her fear and she raced to Dermot. His eyes flickered open to catch her own, horror etched on his handsome features. Then, *he* flickered. His entire body, in and out of view.

Emrysa slammed to a halt, her toes a whisper away from the blooded sign on the ground.

She spun to Nimue, who's face contorted into glee.

"It's not him." Emrysa said in disbelief. "It's... it's a trick."

Nimue slow-clapped. "I very nearly had you, didn't I?" She clicked her fingers and the image of Dermot disappeared leaving an empty space but, an empty space in which Emrysa knew was made for her.

"What sort of dark art is this?" Emrysa spat, feeling now the power of the mark seeping from the bloodied pentagon. She felt the pull of her soul ebb toward it but fought it all the same. Emrysa flicked her fingers outward, casting an attack spell at Nimue, who caught it with a deathly smile and returned the gesture. Emrysa ducked, and side stepped, careful not to step a foot into the pentagon, then threw a fire spell creating a flaming wall between them. Then, as fast as she could, Emrysa fled.

She had to find her brother, no matter what. Nimue did not pursue, and instead, stayed behind the walls of flame laughing a cool and measured laugh. "You think so much of yourself that you would believe to woo me as you did Merlin, you pathetic, vain, creature!"

Emrysa ignored Nimue's voice that chased her along the cavernous corridors. She could see the sliver of light ahead, braced her eyes for the shock of light and all but threw herself from the cave.

Half blinded by the light, she scrabbled to Bruce who whinnied. He started pulling back from the tree he was tied upon in panic, eyes wide with fear. The leather reins stretched but did not snap. She managed to calm Bruce long enough to untie him, mount, and swing around when the spell came.

It pelted the horse with so much force, he screamed, rearing as high as possible. Emrysa gripped his neck. His scream cut short. His warm muscular neck turned to hard stone beneath her touch. The horse's entire body solidified.

"Shit!" Emrysa slid from the now stone horse, falling to the ground with a thump and then another blow struck.

This time hitting Emrysa.

This time pounding not only her body.

This time, turning all she knew into blackness.

24

POWER AND MAGIC

*T*he chants echoed in the great expanse, the voices ringing back and repeating the call again and again.

Old words.

Strange words.

Words that should not be spoken.

Her head hurt, and it took several long seconds for Emrysa's sight to focus, to lose its blurred edges. She made to rub her eyes, but her found her wrists were bound behind her back. That's when the pain hit. She groaned and tried to gather herself from the cold, wet ground to her knees, but she couldn't maintain the energy needed. She collapsed, a loud crack as her head hit the ground with a splash upon her face—a metallic twang of warm blood splattered across her lips.

In a haze, her head spinning, her eyes followed the sound of the chorus.

The Alchive Council—and leading the chants, Nimue.

The double-crossing bitch!

The entire escape plan had been a trick. The Council had always known she would come here, she knew this as true as her own heartbeat. They didn't follow her here, instead she had stupidly followed their orders.

Emrysa groaned as she struggled once again to her knees, resting upon forearms and elbows, she tried to shuffle forward, but the confines of the blood-smeared pentagon kept her in place. She could not escape its boundary, held within the grips of the black-flamed candles.

This was a dark art—something the Alchive Council should never condone. But they no longer resembled the Council kept in place to protect. Not with their floor-length black hooded cloaks that all but concealed their faces in shadow, deer skull headdresses with ornate antlers sharpened and bejeweled.

On they chanted.

"Why?" Emrysa sobbed, as a whisper at first, then finding the strength of her voice. "*Why?*"

Only Nimue broke the chant and stepped forward

from the congregation. "Power," she said simply. "Power and magic."

"But you know, you know I've done nothing to deserve this condemnation, nothing!"

"Did you not use a soul spell? A dark art? Did you not create a portal into another world? Bring its darkness into ours? Kill you parents? Your entire staff?" Nimue asked sweetly.

"You were *there.* That's not all true, you know it, you were there." Emrysa looked into the deep eye sockets of the deer skulls covering Nimue's face, hoping to reach the eyes beneath. "That's not how things happened!"

The chants continued. Louder now. The congregation stepped forward.

Nimue reached into her cloak and pulled out a book. A book of shadows. The *Cheval* Book of Shadows. Seeing it in her hands, it was wrong, all wrong. Emrysa sobbed. She knew how bad this looked, *the blood spells* she thought, chastising herself for the madness that allowed her to create those things in the first place.

"Emrysa, we have to rid the world of you and your power, of what you may become." Nimue whispered now, crouching just inches away from the blood-smeared pentagon that was her prison. "We cannot allow you to become what you may. We cannot allow your bloodline to take magic away from this world."

"Nimue, *please.* Why are you doing this to me? Why?"

"Because *I* want the Cheval power in *my* hands."

Nimue clicked her fingers—black flames flickered from her fingertips. *The killing spell,* Emrysa thought and her only thought was the fear that her brother may fall to the same fate.

And as if thoughts could summon, he appeared.

"Emrysa!" Dermot yelled as he reached the dark heart of the cave, beside him, the young maid Rhian. Merlin closed in behind, skidding to a halt, frozen at the sight.

"What *is* this?!" Merlin raged. Emrysa had half a notion to be a least a little thankful that none of this was his doing. That he, too, had not double-crossed her. Nimue wasted no time and cast a spell as quick as lightning that crashed into Merlin's chest and this time, he really did freeze to the spot, his red aura disappearing completely in Nimue's stranglehold. Dermot managed to miss the blow, but it was enough to trigger something in Emrysa, something primal.

Despite the forces of magic holding her, she roared, bracing herself as the pain came, bracing herself as she breached the invisible barrier stained with blood.

Bracing herself as the last fiber of her soul split and tore away from her body completely.

DIVIDED

*S*ome pain can be described, it can be sensed. The pain of grief, the pain of heartbreak, betrayal, or the severing of a limb. There is an understanding of its depth and of its healing, and of time and place.

This is not what a full severing of the soul feels like.

It was as if the universe exploded inside her chest—stars, comets, worlds, black holes—all pushing themselves against the containment of her body. An excruciating torture as if she would erupt from the inside out. She howled, a sound belonging to the very pits of hell buried beneath their feet. The blood-spell prison erupted into blackened flames, smoke swirling through the dank air. Emrysa writhed, jolting with agonizing movements.

"Emrysa!" Dermot yelled. Rhian clung to him, tears dripping down her youthful face.

She tried to reply. She wanted to say something, *anything* that would make her brother believe the torture was not as bad as it looked. A lie. The biggest lie and she felt her sinews tear, her bones crunch. She tried, but when she opened her mouth, a colossal scream emanated.

The sound blasted everyone from her. Like felled trees they crashed to the ground.

The Alchive Council staggered to their feet, reformed, Nimue at its front.

Emrysa welcomed death now. Welcomed an end to the insufferable pain the blood prison caused when she broke through its barrier.

As if Nimue knew her thoughts—and of course, she did, Emrysa remembered her mind probing since their very first encounter—Nimue cast. Yet instead of the death spell, she sent only more pain. A torture spell. The darkest of incantations.

Emrysa should have passed out with the pain, she knew it. Nobody could withstand this much suffering and still live. But Nimue was *keeping* her alive. Keeping her alive to feel it all.

"Stop!" yelled one of the Council members. He threw off the deer scull headdress and whipped down his hood to expose his wizened face, his wild grey hair and flowing beard. "This is beyond us, Nimue. Stop. It's barbaric!"

"Shut up, Ffroth!" Nimue yelled. "Or you'll suffer the same result."

The young pretty witch seen from the scrying board also threw off her mask in disgust. Several other members followed suit and discarded their ceremonial wear, removing their masks to expose faces ingrained with disgust and unease.

"We did not come here for this disgusting show, Nimue," Ffroth roared. "We came for the prophecy, to *save* the future of magic. If this is what it takes to do so, then magic would be better off dead. Stop, I command you. There is another way!"

Ffroth cast toward Nimue, but as he did, so did many of her followers, creating a safe barrier around her.

"Bloody magic," Ffroth scoffed, and reached into the folds of his gown for a tiny vial of bubbling liquid. He threw it at Merlin, the glass smashed before his feet, green smoke rising to undo the spell Nimue had place upon him. Ffroth gave a satisfied nod. "You can always rely on silence," Ffroth muttered to himself, already knowing Merlin would have what it took to help stop Nimue's wrath.

"Emrysa!" Merlin yelled, now alive with rage.

Dermot, Ffroth, Merlin, the young witch, and several Council members who had discarded their robes, now cast at Nimue, splitting the Alchive Council into two. Nimue's followers continued to cast a safe barrier of protection over her, relishing in the pain and torture the powerless Emrysa lived.

And Emrysa watched it all with acute clarity, the spell working on her senses to feel everything. *Everything* in vivid detail. Which was how she noticed the turning of Nimue's fingertips. Her deep inhale before she changed her spell. The slant of her shoulders that told Emrysa exactly where Nimue would cast. Emrysa's bloodshot eyes turned to her brother. To Merlin. The old man and the Council members trying to help her. Rhian, the maid so like her younger sister, helpless and powerless, hiding behind a small rock.

Nimue was going to kill them all.

Anticipating the exact moment Nimue would turn her spell around with the acuteness of the details the prissy pale bitch had bestowed upon her, Emrysa dug deep. She combined all her pain, all her torture, all her fear. All her lost hopes. Lost dreams. The million details of her future life that now lay broken beneath her feet. All of it, she hauled it into one last spell.

A spell of protection.

To protect the ones she loved. To protect the ones capable of loving *her*.

In a flash, Nimue spun to her left. Emrysa dropped to the floor, but before the relief of pain leaving her body could be felt, she cast.

The protection spell flew from her hands with one agonizing yell, hurtling toward her tribe. It would reach them before Nimue's spell. Emrysa's smile quickly melted away with the sound of the whirling Darkness.

It had found them. Empowered by the faerie roads. It had found them all.

Just as Emrysa's protection spell hit its intended targets, so the black mass roared into the heart of the chamber, belching acrid smoke and covering the walls with mold and decay, its thundering boom deafening. It caught Emrysa's protection spell and morphed it. The glittering gold shimmering on her targets now glittered with black. Dermot, Merlin, Rhian, the old man first to stand up for her, the young pretty witch who quickly followed, half of the Alchive Council who tried to help her, suddenly gasped in pain. Their hands shooting to their collar bones as blackened smoke swirled from between their clasped fingers. When they released their hands, it was not protection spell placed upon them, but instead, a dark mark etched upon their skin.

Two crescent moons back-to-back.

Just like the sign Emrysa had seen on her dead parents' chamber door.

Screams rang out. The Darkness would kill them. Kill them all.

Succumb to me, it whispered in Emrysa's mind. She would never. *Never.*

Succumb to me and in return I shall pardon their lives.

The world stopped turning. She watched everything in slow motion.

I have to do this, don't I? She asked herself. *I have to do this. Succumb to the Darkness to save the ones I love.*

She stole one more glance at her brother, whose kind heart propelled him to risk his life as he pulled Rhian crying from her hiding place before the Darkness got to her. He yelled out for *her*, for Emrysa, all the while. She watched Merlin, desperately trying to hold back the Darkness with the help of the old man and the pretty young witch, but no matter their magical prowess, the Darkness was too much. She could see the strain on Merlin's face, see it in the way his weakening hands shook with exertion.

Perhaps there's a way I can control the Darkness if it's within me. If I succumb. Perhaps I can shape it. Stop it from spreading. Contain *it?*

She closed her eyes and opened her arms—and her heart—to the Darkness.

26

LACED WITH DEATH

*I*t hurtled toward her, all rage and excitement, just as it had when Emrysa first encountered the Darkness in the blackened forest.

Fear caused her bowels to weaken, a hot trail of urine scolding her inner thighs. It was coming. It was coming.

"No!" roared Merlin.

Their eyes locked in one pain-ridden, desperate stare that spoke a million apologies and love songs in less than a moment. He raised his hands to his heart. He mimed the words, *I'm sorry*, and with his hands in a circular motion, threw a spell at her.

It was laced with black.

It was laced with death.

It *was* the death spell.

Her face dropped; dread replaced by sorrow. Her last breath forced itself from her lungs with her dismay.

Merlin was trying to kill her.

I cannot let the Darkness take you, my love, Merlin whispered in her mind, even so, his voice broke, she felt his sobs. *I will keep you alive... in my heart.*

The Darkness and the death spell hit Emrysa together, in perfect unison.

And there was nothing.

27

CHOICES

*D*ying was like a dream. All the fear disappeared, and Emrysa was left with nothing but an all-knowing calm.

There was darkness, but not the darkness of dread, but instead the absence of anything.

There was nothing but a cool, dark calm.

Ahead, in the distance, a light began to glow and flicker with a pale shimmer.

She walked toward it.

Curious.

As she did, images played to the left and the right of her, larger than life, as if life was happening on a huge screen. Moving pictures before her eyes.

Some made her stop and ponder.

Some she walked by without a second glance.

None made her feel anything other than... curious.

Emrysa, what was *once* Emrysa, stopped as one scene faded and abstract images began to play.

A raven's amber eye.

A hilt of a sword.

Hands as old as time clasped around a slender neck.

Curious.

She continued.

Then another cascade of images caused her to pause.

A flame-haired maiden with fire in her heart.

A winter-skinned girl with a dragon in her soul.

A reflection of Emrysa, but not *Emrysa staring sadly at a golden pendant in her hand.*

Curiouser.

She continued toward the light. To her right, a dark army raged. To her left, a wicked secret lay buried.

She kept walking.

She reached the light and waited. It seemed like the right thing to do.

A voice, a whisper, a wise tone spread around.

The Darkness is coming. We have not much time. Will you fight the Darkness? Or, will you harness it? The choice is yours.

Emrysa listened to the options without emotion, and simply wondered, *will I fight it, or will I harness it?*

There was a hiss, and Emrysa turned to her left. A

small puncture appeared in the nothingness, and through it a darker shadow began to spool.

The Darkness is coming, the voice whispered more urgently.

When Emrysa turned back to the front, bearing in mind the small hiss of shadows, she noticed two marble plinths awaiting her. Each with a large crystal sat atop. She knew she had to touch them. And so she did.

One was orange. The other yellow.

Not much difference between the two.

Do not be fooled, your next choice has the ability to change the world.

Emrysa held each in turn, knowing what would happen if she decided to walk back into the light. Two very different futures laid themselves out before her.

Will I fight it, or will I harness it?

The hiss of shadow began to spread, and an idea of urgency brushed her mind as softly as a butterfly's wing.

I must choose now.

Yes, you must. There isn't any time.

Can I stay here? Emrysa asked, curious.

If you wish.

Emrysa considered the futures. Considered her choices. Considered the havoc each future could cause.

Is there another choice? Emrysa asked.

There are always choices.

Calmly, Emrysa picked up the orange crystal, then, almost as an afterthought, also picked up the yellow crystal, and slowly walked into the pale blue light, leaving the place behind her to crumble to dust as if it had never existed.

RAVEN HEART

*H*er first inhale back into life seared her lungs with burning pain. The force of life, heart, and soul hit her, bombarding her with memories and emotions, and something else she couldn't quite place.

Whereas moments before everything and every thought seemed so calm, now the torrent of feelings overwhelmed her.

The choice she had made paralyzed her with fear.

She knew what was coming.

A heavy, *heavy,* burden lay ahead.

She felt hot, clammy. More than hot. On the ground she began to itch at her skin, tearing at her leather clothes.

She rose, screaming, wild like a banshee. Her skin. Her *skin!*

She didn't notice everybody around hover into a protective stance. Two separate groups of the Alchive Council. All she could think about was the burning sensation in her veins. With a flash of magic, she stripped herself of her clothes, marveling at the power in her hands.

"She has the Darkness within her, you insolent fools!" Nimue called out. "She has the power of worlds and danger in her blackened heart. Look!"

And look they did, to Emrysa's naked body, snaking with black vines toward her heart. And over the sacred heart-space, a huge, sprawling dark mark inked itself upon the canvas of her body. Veins like the reaching tendrils in the darkened forest branching ever out.

"We must kill her again before she realizes her full power!" Nimue ordered and half of the Alchive Council prepared their spells.

The other half looked on helplessly to the crying, inconsolable Dermot. The young pretty witch who soothed him, the magicless girl hovering from one agitated foot to the other, and the steadfast Ffroth. Merlin had already left, disappearing in the instant he cast his killing spell toward the love of his life.

"Kill her, kill her now." Nimue's small tribe cast, and

the combined spell pummeled into Emrysa who did nothing but laugh.

A sly smile crept over her face. "You know *nothing!*" Emrysa sneered. She threw her arms outwards and a thousand ravens burst forth from her heart space, cawing into the dank cave. She threw her head back and laughed a sad, pitiful laugh.

Nimue's tribe tried again.

"Don't," Dermot sobbed, "*please*, don't kill her. Don't kill her. I can't lose her again."

But they cast anyway. This time sparks of black flame danced around Emrysa, swirling as angrily as the Darkness had before.

"There's another way. A way to contain her," Ffroth said.

"Then let's do it," Dermot spat. "If it means it will give us time to work out what to do then let's do it."

"Oh!" said Ffroth wearily. "It will give us time, all right. Too much time. What do you know of alchemy, young man?"

"Rather a lot," Dermot said.

"Good." Ffroth threw him several vials from the folds of his robe and Dermot knew of their power at once.

"I'm sorry, sister," Dermot yelled. "I'm sorry."

He smashed the vial on the floor, Ffroth threw his in the same place and the chemicals mixed and swelled.

"We need a combined effort. We need a holding spell. All of you, Nimue, that goes for you too."

And they threw their spells toward Emrysa. She didn't even try to stop them. She just locked eyes with Dermot, watching as the blue glow lit up his face, reminding her of only hours earlier when he chased her down the corridors laughing into the winter sun.

She smiled, full of pity and pain and *pride*—full of courage and bravery and her deepest, darkest fears. Emrysa knew it would be a long, long, time before she would see his face again. She knew her incarceration would hollow out her returned heart and soul in the time it would take. She was full of knowing...

Knowing her name would be spoken with harsh lies, spite, and harsher half-truths.

Knowing the rumors would grow to legends based on nothing but hidden secrets.

But also knowing, that one day, her time would come.

The spelled raced toward her; it *was* coming. She smiled and called out over the chorus of witches' incantations, "The Darkness is coming, and the moon-marked will rise."

She had no idea how twisted her last words would become in the long slow, centuries she knew she would have to endure...

PART III

"When we finally realize that the truth doesn't exist, but rather, it is molded to our own perception of reality, marred by our own memories and emotions, and the passing of time—only then, will we begin to truly see."
–Emrysa Cheval

29

A NEW PERSPECTIVE

The images dissolved leaving nothing but the whiteness of The Void.

Emrysa took a theatrical bow, low and elegant like a ballerina. She stood, slowly, gracefully.

"And so, you see."

Amara and Fae stared, mouths open, as Emrysa's memories faded from their own.

"Well don't stand there catching flies!" she barked.

Fae was the first to speak. Her eyes rimmed red, perhaps because she sensed Emrysa's loss of the dragon heart the most. "All this time. All this time you've been trying to *help?*"

"Oh, don't be so gullible, sister," Amara barked, suddenly realizing quite how similar she was to her aunt. "This is just *her* version of the truth. Doesn't make it's real."

Emrysa slow clapped. "Bravo, bravo. You're not as stupid as you look." She smirked at the irony. "But still, the time has come for you to choose."

"To choose what?" Amara asked.

"To choose sides."

Amara and Fae shared a worried glance.

"Choose wisely," Emrysa said, then, with a roll of her eyes, "Because how many times have I had to say, *the bloody Darkness is bloody coming!*" She blew out hard and regathered her calm. "So, back to my original question. Are you going to help me fight the Darkness or not?"

She was met with silence. All around The Void began to drip away, the truth spell having completed its incantation. The hall around them suddenly vibrant and busy and chaotic.

Fae nodded, biting her lip as she thought. She looked around at the crowds standing dumbstruck. How long had passed? Moments? Hours? *Seconds?* Had everyone else experienced Emrysa's memories too?

"I will fight," Fae said, feeling the truth in her bones. "I'll fight against the Darkness with you."

She stepped forward to Emrysa's side, and Hemeth was quick to follow.

"I too," said another voice in the crowd and then another.

Emrysa, instead of looking pleased, seemed bored. As if she knew this would happen all along but still had to play the part to get everybody else to catch up. She scanned the crowds for Dermot's face, only then did a crease of sadness emerge at her ruby red lips.

Many more witches joined Emrysa. Amara still stood steadfast.

"Well, what are you waiting for you stupid girl?" Emrysa said, exasperated.

Amara hissed, yet stepped forward to join Fae at Emrysa's side, taking a side glance at Bedivere in his compelled state as she did.

"Perfect timing!" Emrysa said, and with that, the large doors of King Arthur's hall swung open.

A dozen elder witches and wizards strode through.

Emrysa smiled.

Fae's heart nearly leapt from her chest. "Mother!" Fae called, watching as their mother headed the march.

As Mother walked the center of the hall, the crowd parting as she did, she morphed. Ageing backwards.

Fae smiled, remembering the first time she had seen her mother in her youth, when they first began their hunt for Emrysa. She saw that youthful version again and her heart swelled with pride. All she wanted was to be embraced, to tell her mother of her dragon heart.

Amara stared emotionless as Mother got closer, her youth regaining with each step. Her serious brow knotted as her mother became younger. And younger still—willowy, lithe, *pale*.

She finally reached them, but instead of acknowledging her daughters, Mother stared disgustedly at Emrysa instead.

"What have you done with Morganne, you *bitch?*" she spat.

Fae flinched at the venom. Amara and Emrysa were prepared for it.

Emrysa smiled, a mean, cruel, spiteful smile. "Nimue. So nice of you to join us."

30

RECLAIMED

*a*mara watched the standoff between her mother and aunt, feeling their brewing storm raging in her bones—not that she needed the strange, deep sensation to alert her. The venom between these old, old enemies leaked from them like the Darkness in Emrysa's memories.

The middle sister cast her serious black eyes over the Alchive Council, the branch of the Council that had condemned Emrysa. Did they know? Did anyone know the truth? Who here was *really* fighting the Darkness? Were they all trying to fight the same demon but somehow got lost along the way? Like a maze of trees blocking the clear path, had they been going around in circles for centuries, when they could have just come together to battle the evil as one?

The evil.

Amara took a moment to study her aunt, they looked so alike—she and this woman whose memory and legend had instilled fear into witches for centuries. She, too, had despised the woman for all she represented, ever since the knowledge of her being came into existence. Emrysa caught her eye, and a flicker of annoyance pinched her features. *Why does she always scowl at me?* Amara thought with her own scowl and almost laughed at their similarities.

A dark mass of shadow passed the windows outside, casting an inky cloud across the hall. It covered half Emrysa's face in shadow and Amara wondered if this was the truth of things. *That we all hold darkness and light within us.*

A maelstrom of thoughts continued to race through Amara's mind.

Her mother, Nimue. How had she won over Dermot?

My gosh, my father, Amara thought in a fractured moment. An unusual warm feeling in her heart swelled for the man she had never known, had refused to get to know, and yet somehow, through Emrysa's memories, a deep sense of kinship brewed. He was a good man. Had Mother influenced him with her purple aura as she had Merlin?

Merlin.

She watched him, his zombie-like appearance staring into nothing with the black, black eyes of the moon-marked army. He looked into emptiness with such profound sadness, Amara wondered if he, too, had relived the past through the truth spell whilst under the compulsion of the moon-mark.

For the briefest of moments, Amara grasped time and space, holding it in her mind. Slowing the world. Slowing her spinning thoughts.

She needed time.

In the brief moment she held the spell between her hands, molding and melding time as she took in the vastness of Camelot Hall—witches and innocents who had seen the truth stood with and gathered around Emrysa readying to battle the Darkness. Opposite, the Alchive Council led by Mother stared back in disgust. Would they fight the Darkness together, or fight against their past grievances and bitter lies?

Beside Emrysa, still moon-marked; King Arthur, Merlin, Kay, and... *and Bedivere.*

Her eyes lingered on him, before a guilty glance to Emrysa, who beneath the surface, trapped, was the beautiful and kind, and very much in love, Morganne.

What an unbearable mess.

In some ways, Amara wanted nothing more than to

return to the old days and the old way, when life was simple. The days before she first stepped out into the Mystic Wood under the command of the full moon, following Shadow into the heart of woods and the heart of Mother's secrets. The days when the sisters were sisters of three, strange but not unusual girls living in a simple cottage tucked away in the country. Days before the Darkness. Days before lies and myths and legends.

Days before the heart-wrenching pain of unrequited love tore at her organs.

With that thought, Amara lost her grip on her spell and the world and time spun once more, jolting her back into reality.

"You planned this moment for centuries." Mother—Nimue—barked. "All this time in your hovel, you planned to trick my daughter, to steal her life-force so I could not kill you on sight."

Emrysa gave a self-congratulatory smile. "It was clear foresight. Something I bet you wish you possessed."

"I don't need foresight to know I'll kill you the first moment I get a chance."

"Only the weak rely on chance, you prissy little wench," Emrysa said with a beatific smile.

Amara watched the sparring witches, then bent

toward her sister. "Do you have any idea what we should do next?" she uttered behind her hand.

Fae's face was as emotionless as the moon when she shrugged and shook her head in a gentle whisper, before jolting.

An almighty, deafening crack whipped the air. The ground of the great hall trembled.

"What the..." Amara started, looking first to Emrysa then to her mother. *Whose spell is this?* But by the confusion on her aunt's face, and the alarm of Mother's, Amara knew this was not their work. This was something else. This was something far, far darker.

Her moon-mark itched, and she cast a warning glare at Emrysa.

"Don't you dare!" Amara yelled, having felt the first stages of the moon-mark call before.

With a violent shake of her head, Emrysa denied its charge.

"It's not me," Emrysa said, looking down and scratching at her own moon-mark scrawled across her body and heart.

"Then tell us what it is, you halfway witch!" Nimue yelled. "You're meant to be the one with foresight. Tell us what's going on!"

"I... I..." Emrysa trailed off as the entire building shook, rocked by the clutches of Darkness screaming outside the great hall. "I don't know. I only saw up to this moment. The moment where everyone agrees to help."

"The Council has *not* agreed," Nimue spat.

Emrysa paused for a beat, all snide and bitterness dripping from her face. "But you must."

The ground grumbled.

Amara turned to Fae, whose winter blue eyes now glowed like amber flames in preparation to morph. "We need to flee," Fae said. "The Darkness is too great, I can feel it in the pit of my stomach."

Beside Fae, Hemeth stepped forward, "What about Lord Cheval?" Hemeth asked. Emrysa jolted at the name—at the use of her *Father's* title used upon her long-estranged brother. Hemeth, with his lilting, lyrical accent continued, "he opened the portal not once, but twice." The otherworldly stranger softened to a lopsided smile and shrugged. "Third time lucky?"

"No!" Emrysa yelled. "We can't run away from this. We must—"

Blackness crashed through the windows to a crescendo of a million shattered shards of glass.

Witches screamed. People screamed. Fae roared. Amara watched on silent as the dark mass whipped around them. It danced, coalesced, morphed, and in a breath—reached for them; grasping with obsidian talons.

Amara felt the pulling, the pulling of her soul, of lung and sinew. Of magic.

"No!" She grappled, fighting back, pulling her magic back into herself.

Mother—Nimue—fell to her knees. Emrysa clutched at her body screaming obscenities into the callous Darkness that swirled and twirled around the witches writhing bodies.

Fae roared, white flames smothered completely by a blacker flame of smoke and bone. Trancelike, Merlin, King Arthur, Kay, and Bedivere—still under Emrysa's moon-mark spell—stood stock still, their widening eyes the only tell of pain.

A laugh older than time penetrated the minds of all. Amara gritted her teeth against the sound, against the pain, against the pulling of her soul. For the briefest of moments, she could nearly grasp the depth of hollowness within Emrysa's soul broken flesh.

The sound grew, a terrible pitch echoing between every organ, every cell. It pulsed within Amara's blood. She dropped to her knees, then with a sudden screaming wail of terror, the Darkness lifted.

Disappeared. Vanishing, and leaving behind an unbearable and somehow terrifying silence.

The silence of anticipation. The silence of waiting. The silence of stalked prey.

Breathless, Amara clutched at her wheezing chest, her eyes finding her younger sister huddled in the redhead's arms. Her mother rose to her feet and Amara didn't know whether to help her or condemn her. Bedivere, *Bedivere,* blinked several times and looked around himself, confused, alongside the others lifting out from their moon-marked trance. But Amara had no time to welcome them back—no time to ask because Emrysa's shriek was enough to stop any thoughts of the Darkness.

"My magic!" she screamed, hysterical. "My magic! It's gone! My..." she clutched her chest. The moon-mark dripped from her skin like spilled ink until it disappeared completely. She cried then smiled, then cried again.

Amara had the sense to know that somehow, with the Darkness taking Emrysa's magic, it also took some of the burdens she had been harboring for all this time—for centuries—to ensure she had the strength for this very moment. She could tell by the way the haunted look in her aunt's eyes ebbed, softened.

So now what?

The Darkness had reclaimed itself.

Was all my aunt's suffering for nothing? Amara thought.

She could not believe it. Something else was stirring, she was sure of it.

"This is why you only saw up to this moment, mmm. Interesting." Nimue mused. "You couldn't see past your life without magic."

"Her life will still be magic," Merlin said. Consciousness fully returned, he stepped toward Emrysa—his face a crumpled apology. The two star-crossed lovers shared such an intensely private and passionate look, full of heartbreak and fragile possibilities, that Amara had to turn away. Without meaning to, her eyes wandered to Bedivere, watching how his face suddenly came alive with joy.

"Morganne!" he called, rushing forward.

31

SPLIT

A cocktail of hope and hopelessness pounded into Amara's heart. *My sister?* She looked around for her, following Bedivere's longing gaze. His eyes pinned on Emrysa.

Amara gasped.

Morganne flickered, like a mirage, for but a breath before morphing back to Emrysa once more.

"I can't hold her, not without magic," Emrysa said.

"What do you mean?" Nimue demanded.

Amara had deeper concerns. "Oh, by the Goddess. Can either of you survive without the other? Without magic?"

Emrysa hesitated and stammered. "I don't know. But there must be a reason for this to happen. It was imperative

I connected with the fire heart. I don't know why, I have never known why, but I would not have gone through all this torture to ensure it would happen if this didn't have significance. The foresight is strong. The future wants itself realized. The future wants itself to happen."

"The future is unwritten," Amara scowled.

Emrysa flickered, her image replaced with Morganne's perfect form, her red curly hair as vibrant as always, her green, green eyes like shining emeralds. "You need to change things," Morganne said, her voice far, far away despite her strong vision.

Amara rushed forward, Bedivere at her side. "Morganne!" Amara yelled, heart exploding.

"No time. You must change things." Morganne's voice was slipping away. Her form flickered back to Emrysa, then back once more, only this time, less vibrant. This time, less real.

"We will," Amara promised, looking back to Fae whose face was wet with tears, then to her mother, who Amara couldn't decide if she still loved or loathed. "We'll change things. We'll work together, we can, I don't know, maybe, go back in time?"

Morganne shook her head. "It is not the past you need to change…"

And she was gone. Emrysa stood stock still and

stunned. Only one eyebrow arched impossibly high on her forehead. "Well… Shit. I didn't see that coming."

Fae's voice broke through the following silence. "How can we change the future without changing the past?"

"We can't," Amara said, resolute, raising her chin and bracing her shoulders back with the confidence of her words. "To go forward in a different way, we must go back."

"Impossible!" Mother—Nimue—yelled. "You cannot go back. You can *never* go back. You change one thing and everything changes from that moment on. Time should not be manipulated. *Ever!* Do you hear me?"

"But," Amara began wondering what the problem of time manipulating could be. Had she not done it countless times herself? "What if we go back to the time when Emrysa went through the portal? Merlin, you could make the spell that allows nothing otherworldly back into our world—the spell you said you should have made in the memories."

"What about not making me get rid of my dragon heart in the first place, you prissy bitch?" Emrysa spat to Nimue full of venom.

"Because," Nimue continued, looking to Amara and Fae in turn. "Change that, and you girls won't exist. Then who would there be to fight the Darkness."

"But the Darkness would not come," Fae said. By her expression, Amara knew Fae understood the same as she. That somehow by changing the past, they may protect the world from the Darkness, but they would forfeit their own existence in the process.

The air suddenly felt heavy in Amara's lungs. *Is this fear, or something else?* She didn't have to wait long for the answer.

The Darkness hadn't finished with them yet.

Beneath their feet, the ground split open.

"Watch out!" Amara yelled as the ground continued reaching and expanding out like veins from its blackened heart. Branching out, separating everyone. Small groups of witches and innocents grappled onto each other as the ground sunk and disappeared around their feet. Debris tumbled into the deepest depths. The ground continued splitting; forming islands, each one getting smaller, and smaller.

Amara gasped, losing her footing. Nearly tumbling with the falling stones.

All around was chaos. Screams and shouts and sobs.

The cracking ground exploded, continuing to split the ground in ever-smaller islands, shutting everyone off from one another. *The Darkness knows how to create weakness,* Amara thought sourly. She turned to Fae—she and otherworldly man, Hemeth, upon their own island.

King Arthur and Merlin on another. With Amara, Kay, and Bedivere, Emrysa and Mother standing together on the last remaining large island.

The ground shuddered again, the crack was coming. Amara could see it.

They couldn't stay here. She needed to cast a spell. She looked around. Other witches had already started spell casting, some failed helplessly, having somehow lost their magic along with Emrysa—though Amara had not time to ponder why or how. Fae morphed, shrieking with a fierce primal call.

Time—Amara couldn't make time standstill. She could neither make time elongate to help her decide what to do, she needed more focus for that, and the world was a blur. Armed only with the knowledge Morganne had shared, *you must change things*, Amara thought only of going backward. Backward despite her mother's concerns. Backward in *retaliation* to her mother's concerns.

Amara pulled at nature, harder than she ever had before until her entire being vibrated with the knowledge of the cosmos.

"Goddess save us from the Dark
From this place we must depart
Travel us through both time and space,
To leave the Darkness, to leave this place."

The spell took hold. Amara felt the eye of the Goddess upon her—observed, tiny, minuscule against the vastness of the universes. Yet still the ground trembled and cracked beneath her feet.

"Amara!" Mother called as the ground sank away, breaking the spell. Both Nimue and Emrysa fell with the tumbling stones.

"Ouff!" Emrysa coughed, as she caught herself on the ledge of the loosening ground, knuckles white, fingers gripping stone. Amara lost her hold of the spell, no longer feeling the pull of time gone by. Interrupted, the spell buzzed, morphed, clung to Amara as she made one split-second choice as her mother and aunt swayed on the precipice, threatening to fall into eternity.

She reached her hand out to help.

She reached her hand out to help, *Emrysa*.

"Amara?" Mother yelled. "You sullen bitch!"

But it was too late. Her voice faded, the hall faded, everything faded as the spell finally grasped itself once more, pulling at lung and sinew.

I will make everyone safe, I will make everyone safe, Amara chanted—prayed, snapping her eyes shut as the sensation of shooting stars and comets sailing through the vastness of space gripped her. It was a feeling she had felt before, the feeling she felt when she first laid eyes on her sister's love, Bedivere.

Bedivere.

His image interrupted the spell in her mind's eye. She couldn't imagine a future without him.

The Future, Amara heard the Goddess repeat in the throes of the spell casting. Velocity changed, and Amara found herself propelled forward at impossible speed until…

It stopped.

Amara was no longer in Camelot.

EPILOGUE

A warm breeze played through Amara's jet-black hair with a heady floral scent of spring —and an unusual sweetness. Bird song whistled and chirped. A rhythmical creak of rope and swing swayed behind her. She opened one eye, then the other.

"Bedivere?" Amara whispered, seeing only him ahead of her, his face twisted in horror. "Are you okay, are you…?" Her words trailed off. He was not staring *at* her, but behind her. She was about to turn around but;

"Where, by the Goddess's tits, have you taken us?" Emrysa croaked, stepping from behind the dumbstruck knight. Emrysa's eyes followed the line behind Amara's shoulder, her ruby lips twitched with a snarl.

Amara held her breath as she turned, inch by inch to the creaking, rhythmical groan behind her.

She staggered backward. Bedivere grabbed her wrist, keeping her from falling to her weakened knees.

It was their feet Amara noticed first. Swaying to the gentle breeze above her head. Then their faces, eyes bulging, thick tongues lolling. Necks jutting at the wrong angle—the thick ropes seeming the only thing to keep their heads attached to their bodies.

Four dead women swinging to the breeze.

No, not women. *Witches.*

"I asked you where have you brought us?" Emrysa asked again. Nobody looked at each other, instead they stared up at the dead hanging from the gallows.

"I lost my concentration somehow in all the commotion. I think we're... I think we're in the future—"

"The future?" Emrysa barked. "You stupid, *stupid* girl. How could you do such a spell? We're doomed. Do you hear me? We. Are. Doomed!" Emrysa paced a circle, talking to herself—perhaps a trait learned through her centuries in solitude. "Great. My magic has gone, and we're stuck in another time. This will not end well." She stopped, looking around herself then once more to Amara. "And where is everyone else?"

Amara bit her lip but before she could reply, Emrysa flickered from view. For a moment Morganne stood in her place. Her vision coming in and out of focus with the breeze. Bedivere made to grab her hand, but found no purchase, grasping instead fresh air.

"Oh dearest sister," Morganne sighed softly. "What have you done?"

Amara stalked to the gallows, not knowing how to answer. She pulled from a nail a letter written in intricate, swirling handwriting. She read it aloud.

"We've been expecting you. Meet us at the White Hart Inn. Be sure to conceal yourselves beneath their cloaks—"

"—Whose cloaks?" Bedivere interrupted.

Amara pointed to the dead swaying bodies. Bedivere recoiled.

"We have little choice," Amara said as she grappled a spell to transfer the cloaks from the bodies onto themselves. But nothing happened.

"What?" Emrysa barked. "Has your magic gone too?"

Amara shook her head. "It's not gone, it's… different. It's weaker, like it doesn't have the strength to pull the threads of the spell together."

"That's because magic is dying." A voice said from behind.

Amara spun. "Who are you?"

The woman smiled the most melancholic smile Amara had ever seen. "I am Anne West. And you, my dear visitors, are not safe."

"Not safe from what?" Emrysa barked.

"The biggest witch hunt history has ever known." Anne's eyes lingered to the four women swaying on the gallows, and Amara had a feeling things were about to get a lot, *lot*, worse.

"Welcome," Anne continued, "to the demise of the witch."

Amara watched as Morganne flickered into view once more. They shared a stare, a longing recognition only felt between those who had shared a womb. No words needed. They knew they were in trouble. Deep trouble. Amara held up the letter to Anne.

"You know of this?" she asked.

Anne nodded and said only one word before turning and walking away, "come."

With only a short pause, Amara, Emrysa, and Bedivere pulled at the cloaks of the dead to conceal themselves, and followed the witch of a future time toward White Hart Inn, and a future yet unwritten.

To be continued...

I'M busy writing the next tale in this saga. Until then, scan the code below to sign up to my Readers Newsletter to keep updated, and get your hooves on a special Witch Hearts inspired Swag Bag full of exclusive gifts and freebies.

ABOUT THE AUTHOR

Angharad Thompson Rees is a multi passionate creative with a Little Whimsey. A screenwriter, comic scriptwriter, poet, illustrator, and author of fantasy novels and creative journals for children and young adults. Weaving strong imagery with poetical prose, Angharad's stories capture the imagination of young and old with her whimsical offerings.

Discover out more at:
www.littlewhimsey.com

ALSO BY ANGHARAD THOMPSON REES

Magic and Mage Series

Witch Hearts

Fire Heart

Dragon Heart

Raven Heart

Middle Grade Adventures

Forever Night

The Snow Pony

Magical Adventures & Pony Tales

The Painted Pony

The Galloping Pony

The Girl and her Pony

The Runaway Pony

The Desert Pony

The Wooden Pony

Published by Little Whimsey 2018
Copyright © 2024 by Angharad Thompson Rees
Edited By Phoenix Editing

Made in the USA
Las Vegas, NV
27 October 2024